ANOTHER BREATH, ANOTHER SUNRISE

MICHAL'S DESTINY SERIES - BOOK 4

USA Today Bestselling Author

ROBERTA KAGAN

ISBN (eBook): 978-1-957207-76-6
ISBN (Paperback): 978-1-957207-77-3
ISBN (Hardcover): 978-1-957207-78-0

Title Production by The BookWhisperer

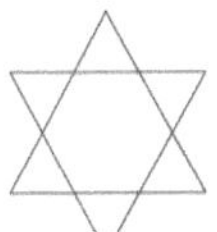

prologue

HITLER'S DREAMS of a Thousand-Year Reich came to an end when the Nazis surrendered to the Allies in 1945.

Adolf Hitler, Eva Braun (his wife of a few hours), Joseph Goebbels with his wife and family, and several other close colleagues had been hiding in Hitler's underground bunker when they learned that Stalin's army was about to enter Berlin.

Rather than face the humiliation of defeat, Hitler and the rest of the group hiding in the bunker committed suicide. But first, they murdered the Goebbels' young children. Even though the door finally slammed shut on the reign of Nazi terror, the world's suffering was not yet over. A bloody war still raged on in the Pacific.

As the Allies began to make their way through the territories that had been previously occupied by the Nazis, they began to liberate the concentration camps. What they found stunned the world.

The horrors that the Third Reich left behind were almost beyond human comprehension—piles of dead bodies, ovens surrounded by ashes consisting of burnt flesh, and gas chambers with small windows for sadistic guards to watch the killings of innocent victims.

The sight was so monstrous that many of the soldiers involved in the liberation said that no matter how hard they tried, they could not erase the images from their minds. And then, those who were still alive, half-starved walking corpses, had witnessed things that would change them forever.

These poor lost souls, Jews and non-Jews, Jehovah's Witnesses, homosexuals, Poles, and prisoners of war, would now come forth from the darkness into the light and somehow begin to look for their loved ones. They had no idea whether their friends and family were alive or dead, and many would never find any information.

These were the survivors. A handful of people who had managed to escape Nazi persecution with little more than their lives. Not only had they lost everything and everyone, but they carried the guilt of being chosen to live while others perished, a haunting syndrome that would come to be known as survivor's guilt. "Why me? Why was I spared when everyone I know and love is dead?"

Their homes and all of their belongings had been confiscated when they were arrested, so now they had no place to live except displaced persons camps. Quite often, Jews who returned to the cities where they'd lived before the war found out that anti-Semitism did not end with the death of the Third Reich. In several villages, Jewish refugees were murdered upon their return by those who had once been their friends and neighbors.

As for the Nazis, some of the high officials like Himmler decided to bite through a cyanide capsule when caught rather than face the consequences of what they'd done. Others tucked their tails between their legs and ran or hid in fear. And the handful of Nazi soldiers who were still left in the city after the surrender were busy hanging deserters in the streets.

The women of Berlin, many of whom were not Nazis but had been afraid to stand up to Hitler, now awaited the Russian army in terror, with no able-bodied men left to defend them. Rumors spread like cancer through Berlin that the Russian army was cruel and had raped and pillaged their way through the German countryside.

Thousands of women in Berlin took their own lives rather than face the Russians, who were bent on seeing the destruction and humiliation of all Germans.

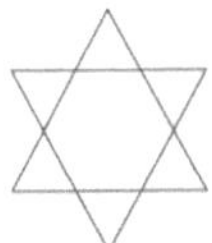

one
Alina

New York
April 1945

ALINA MARGOLIS WOKE up nauseated from the sedative Dr. Stallwarth had given her the night before. She had been terribly distraught and unable to sleep when she'd learned that her dear friend and perhaps the only man she'd ever really loved, Ugo Blok, had enlisted in the army and was fighting somewhere in the Pacific.

Dr. Stallwarth was one of her best friend Klara's regular clients. Klara was a prostitute who was employed in the brothel that Alina owned, and had turned out to be the best friend Alina had ever known. However, she had come into Alina's life from the most unlikely places… Klara was Ugo's ex-wife.

Alina had seen Ugo for the first time on the ship when she and her lover, Johan, were on their way to America from Germany. Johan and Alina had left Germany because of the Nuremberg laws forbidding the marriage between Aryans and Jews. Johan was Lotti's brother. Lotti and her husband, Lev, had been friends of Alina's parents. Lev was Jewish, but Johan and Lotti were not. Johan had fallen head over heels in love with Alina the first time he saw her. Then, with the climate in Germany, as the Nazis were rising in power, Johan had convinced Alina to leave and go to America.

On that voyage, Alina met Ugo, who was traveling alone from Russia to America. He was to meet up with his wife, Klara. There was an instant attraction between Ugo and Alina, but because they were committed to other people, neither of them ever acted upon it.

Then Johan died of an infection on the ship, leaving Alina pregnant, and alone to fend for herself in a strange land. She'd tried to make it on her own, but it was impossible. She hardly spoke English and had very little money.

Circumstances had forced her to find Johan's estranged father, Trevor, who had abandoned Johan and his mother before Johan was born. Trevor was wealthy, older, and widowed, and Alina was young and beautiful. Nature took its course. He became attracted to her, and they married. But their reasons for marrying were very different.

He'd married her for her youth and beauty; she'd married him to secure a home for her unborn child. Then, once Joey, Alina's son, was born, Trevor changed. He was an old man with no patience for a child. He was annoyed at the noise and disruption in his house. Trevor had never been a kind man, but he became abusive. Alina was miserable.

When Ugo arrived in America, he found that Klara, his young wife who had come to the United States to live the American dream, wasn't satisfied with the life of poverty that he, an immigrant, could provide.

To his dismay, she began selling her body. They had been childhood sweethearts. They had been raised on farms, but America had changed Klara. She wanted more out of life, and eventually, she moved into a brothel, leaving Ugo feeling like less of a man.

Ugo was physically very strong. He needed work, so he began working for a company moving furniture. One day, when he was transporting a piano to a home in an upscale neighborhood, he recognized Alina. He called out to her and she was glad to see him. He didn't want to say goodbye, so he thought of a way to see Alina again —Ugo had begun taking English classes, and he casually suggested she join him. She agreed, so they began to attend class together once a week.

Alina and Ugo had been secretly in love since the day they met, although they had never been able to get past their pride and accept their feelings for each other. The final blow was when Ugo found out about Alina's decision to open a brothel. But Alina needed financial security to take care of her son, Joey, who had survived polio, and she was unable to find work. Then, one afternoon, she'd run into Klara.

Alina had a little money put away. When her wealthy husband Trevor became abusive, she began stealing money from him in hopes of one day escaping his violent temper. When Alina saw Klara, she thought that Klara would be resentful of her relationship with Ugo. But Klara had no lingering interest in Ugo; instead, Klara explained to Alina that it would be good for both of them if she took her money and invested it in a brothel.

Alina explained that she would not be willing to work as a prostitute, but Klara said that she had friends in the business who would be grateful to work for a good madam, a fair madam. If Alina opened the house, Klara would have a clean, safe place to work with an honest boss, and Alina would have the financial security she needed. And so it was Klara who had helped Alina to find, negotiate, and buy the house that would become a refuge for both of them.

It was a large wooden structure, old and solid looking, located in the Wallabout neighborhood in Brooklyn near the Navy Yard. It was not the nicest of areas, but because it was not in the middle of Manhattan, the clients, many of whom were married or held important positions, felt more comfortable about not being seen coming or going.

The doctor had been visiting with Klara when Alina had received the news about Ugo. They'd all been in the main living room when Alina told Klara. Stallwarth saw Alina's distress and offered the medicine to help Alina calm her nerves. After the doctor gave her the sedative, she lay in bed and thought about Ugo. He was a good friend, and he loved her.

She'd never doubted that, but independence was more important to Alina than love. That was because she'd lost so many people in her life and then made the mistake of marrying Trevor. When Joey was born, and Trevor had been physically violent to both her and her child, she vowed to herself that she would never allow anyone to have this much control over her life again. That was when she'd begun stealing money from Trevor until she had enough cash hidden away to open the brothel. Ugo had begged her to marry him, to give up the idea of owning a whorehouse and be his wife. But she was not willing to do that. Even though she was a madam and not a prostitute, he was repulsed by her business. And so their friendship had come to a painful and bitter end.

Then, a few weeks before Christmas in 1941, the United States of America was attacked and bombed by the Empire of Japan, which was part of the Axis with Germany and Italy. That was when America entered the war. Men were enlisting left and right, and business slowed down. From what Alina read of the news, things were improving for the Allies as far as the European front was concerned. Hitler was losing the war. It looked like Germany was going to surrender any day now. However, the war against the Japanese raged on in the Pacific.

Then, men began coming home wounded and maimed. They came to the brothel and talked to the girls. From them, Alina learned that the Japanese were brutal enemies. And now, Ugo was off fighting somewhere in the Pacific. Would he die on a battlefield in a country far away without ever knowing her true feelings for him? And if he came home, would she ever tell him? Probably not. But her heart ached with fear and love for him, fear and love she would keep like a sad and bitter secret locked up inside of her, never to be shared with anyone.

▭

The morning light filtered through the small opening in the shades. It was only a thin flicker of light, but it was enough to burn Alina's eyes and aggravate her headache. So, she forced herself out of bed and went into the bathroom to splash her face with cold water. Perhaps that would help.

Downstairs, newspapers lay on the kitchen table, surrounded by cheap earrings, dirty dishes, discarded bras, and clothing that needed washing. Two of the girls had already begun arguing about something. Cigarette smoke mingled with the smells of fresh baking biscuits and rich coffee. Coffee was rationed, but it was given to Klara as a gift by one of her influential clients, who had plenty of black market connections. The girls were not all awake yet. They had just begun trickling downstairs to the kitchen. One of the girls lit a cigarette and put her feet on the table.

"No feet on the table when I am serving breakfast, you hear?" the cook said, and the girl put her feet down.

"Oh shit, would you look at that," Gloria said. She was one of the newest girls. "Now that's a God damn shame." She squinted as she picked up the newspaper. Only a few of the girls could read, so only a few even bothered to look at the paper.

"Hush. Don't take God's name in vain," Maggie said. She was a prostitute, but she wore her cross and worshiped at the church without fail every Sunday. She was a good girl with a kind heart, and no one ever pried or asked her any questions about her religious beliefs.

"Well, it is a shame. Here, look…" Gloria said, handing the newspaper to Maggie. "Oh yeah, that's right, you can't read it. Give it here. Let me read it to you." Gloria read from the newspaper. "It says here that President Franklin D. Roosevelt died of a brain aneurysm last night."

Alina had wrapped her robe around her body. She was just entering the kitchen when she heard Gloria reading the news. It was like a cannon had been fired into her brain. Immediately, her eyes fell upon her three-year-old son, Joey, who sat on the floor playing with a toy.

He was so quiet since he'd recovered from the polio. An image flashed across her mind of Joey having an aneurysm, just like FDR. *Stop it. The US president was old, and Joey is just a child.* Then she looked at her son again and shivered. How could she ignore his twisted body and his limp arm?

The polio had taken so much away from Joey and, at the same time, so much from her as well. Alina gripped the chair and eased herself into it. Roosevelt was dead from a brain aneurysm. An aneurysm can happen at any age to anyone. Could it have been from his bout with polio so many years ago? Could something like this be lying dormant inside of her poor Joey's brain? She thought about this, and she was barely able to breathe. Dear God. Roosevelt had been alive yesterday. Someone said good morning to her, but she didn't answer. She picked up the paper and read more about what had happened. It said that the president complained of a headache, and then within a few hours, without any real warning, he was dead!

Joey, my God, that could happen to Joey. Alive one day, gone the next.

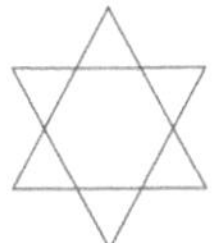

two
Lotti

Berlin
April 1945

LOTTI CHEWED on her lower lip and then gasped as she looked out the third-floor window of her small flat. The section called Kreuzberg, where she lived, had been brutally hit, leaving mass destruction when the bombs rained down on Berlin. The building where Lotti lived was still standing, but parts of the structure were now broken.

Of the twelve apartments in the building, only three remained intact, and Lotti's was one of them. No longer could one hear the sounds of the huge railway station in the distance because the Anhalter Bahnhof had been shattered in a daylight raid when the US Air Force had attacked the heart of the city in February.

For the last several weeks, the women left behind in Germany had cowered in fear of the day when the Russian army would march into Berlin. That day had arrived. From where she stood, she could see the bedlam in the streets.

Berlin, the once beautiful, cosmopolitan city, now lay in ruins from the bombings. The streets were strewn with rubble. Even bodies of dead animals that had to be shot when they escaped from the zoo still littered the pavement. White flags of surrender hung from many of the windows; Lotti knew that the women inside hoped that the flags would somehow inspire the invaders to take pity on them.

There was no point in going to work at her job at the hotel switchboard anymore. All the phone lines were down. In fact, all communication, transportation, and news of the outside world had halted abruptly. There was nothing to do but hide and pray. This was what Hitler had done to Germany. From what Lotti had heard, the Soviets had raped most of the women in the German countryside on their way into Berlin.

Her hand trembled as she pulled the shade closed. Bernadette, her friend, lay asleep in her bed. She was still weak from the botched abortion she'd gone through without ever telling anyone she was pregnant. She would have given everything to be able to bear a child. But it was not meant to be, and even though she'd wished to be a mother more than she could ever express, she would never have that joy.

Berni never said who the father was, and Lotti didn't pry. But Lotti knew that if Berni was sure she wanted an abortion, she could have probably found a doctor willing to put in a claim that either she or the child's father had a genetic disease. That would have made aborting the baby legal, and although Lotti didn't approve of the abortion under any circumstances, at least Berni could have avoided a back-street butcher. Abortions were legal for anyone who had any disorder that could taint the German race. Still, Lotti looked at Berni lying in her bed, breathing softly and shook her head. Lotti couldn't imagine any woman in the world not wanting to have a baby.

What a strange girl Berni was. She was secretive and hard to understand. There were unspoken boundaries with Berni. Lotti was always afraid to ask too many questions about Berni's past. She was afraid she would push her away. Berni rarely volunteered any information about herself.

Lotti first met Berni when Lotti worked on a switchboard at a hotel. Berni was working in housekeeping. Rumors spread among the hotel employees that Lotti had been married to a Jew, so very few people wanted to befriend her. Berni was different. She hardly spoke and never discussed her past, but one day, she befriended Lotti by joining her in the cafeteria.

After a couple of weeks, Berni had agreed to come to dinner at Lotti's apartment. Lotti had gone out of her way to help Berni move from her job in housekeeping to a position on the switchboard. It wasn't a wonderful promotion, but answering phones was easier than scrubbing toilets.

The two women were far apart in age. Berni was in her early twenties, while Lotti was in her late thirties. Still, they became good friends. Sometimes, they would have lunch together in the park. Then, one afternoon, Berni passed out while they were walking through the park. Lotti called for help, which resulted in Lotti finding out that Berni had had a botched abortion. After Berni's hospital stay, Lotti asked if she wanted to come home with her, and Berni said yes. Berni needed help, and Lotti was lonely and needed a friend.

▭

If Bernadette had been able to move freely, Lotti would have taken her to hide in the subway tunnels as many other women had done. But in Berni's condition, that would be impossible. There was no other choice; they would have to stay where they were and await whatever might befall them.

The city was buried in rubble from the earlier bombings. Fire and smoke now filled Berlin, but this time, it was from the Soviet attack as they entered. The world outside Lotti's window was a battle zone. She felt her heart beat fast and her stomach twist and turn, unable to settle because she knew that if the Russians came and broke down the door, they were finished. There was no place to go, no place to hide. All she and Berni could do was beg for mercy.

Peeking out the window, she saw Russian soldiers laughing as they shot defeated German soldiers attempting to surrender, leaving dead bodies and pools of dark blood in their wake. Some of the Russians

were chasing women, pushing them to the ground or against buildings and forcing themselves on them. Every so often, a woman would
cry out, begging to be spared. *Don't vomit*, Lotti told herself, but terror
plunged through her stomach like the blade of a dull knife.

Lotti walked away from the window and dropped into a chair,
putting her head in her hands. The world was upside down, and for
her, nothing would ever be right again.

For months, Dr. Goebbels had promised the German people that
everything would be fine; he'd lied and told them that Stalin would
never get into Berlin. But now, things had taken a downward spiral
for the women left behind.

The powerful Führer, with all of his manipulation and lies, and
Goebbels, his minister of propaganda, another liar, were dead. They'd
committed suicide. Bastards, all of them, she thought, biting her nail.

The Third Reich had destroyed her life, murdered her one and
only love, her Jewish husband, Lev, and taken away all of her close
friends. Even her brother was gone. And now that the Nazis faced
defeat, the cowards took the easy way out, leaving the poor defense-
less women of Berlin to suffer the consequences of their actions.

Just last week, Lotti had heard about the suicide of two young
women who lived upstairs in her apartment building. Lotti had met
them several times, but because of the gossip about her being married
to a Jew, they had rejected her friendship. From what she knew, the
two women had moved in together to save rent money while waiting
for their husbands to return from battle. When they, like so many
others, had learned that the Russians were on their way, they both left
notes to their husbands, telling them they would rather die than be
raped by the invading army.

At first, night hovered like a cloud and then finally fell over the city,
casting a dark shadow over the broken ruins of Berlin. There were no
lights, and Lotti glanced over to the small pile of firewood that they
used for the stove. Soon, she would have to go out and try to cut more.

Last week, she'd paid a large sum to a young boy to purchase a small amount of wood. He'd chopped up a tree in the park, and although he had overcharged her, Lotti was glad to have found him, or she would have had to chop it herself. Now, the pile was dwindling, and soon, she would have to find wood again.

At least it wasn't the dead of winter. They could survive without firewood for a while if need be. But not without water. Lotti walked over to the bucket where she kept their supply. It was getting low as well. There was no running water, no luxury of a bath. Still, they needed the water to drink. So, regardless of the threat posed by the invaders, when their water supply ran out, she would have to find a way to go two blocks to the street fountain to pump another bucketful.

It was hard to believe that before Hitler came into power, Berlin had been a thriving city—a center of art, science, and culture. What would become of her now? Lotti had no idea what the future held. She wished she could talk to Lev. He had such a calming way. "Dear God," she said aloud, her voice more of an angry accusation than a prayer. "Why? Why did you have to let them take Lev?"

Lotti was too nervous and couldn't stay seated. She got up and went into the bedroom to check on Bernadette, who was still asleep. Gently, Lotti pulled the blanket up and covered her friend. It had been a long day. If only she could get a little rest, Lotti thought, as she went to the bed she had once shared with her precious late husband and lay down still wearing her day clothes. She was afraid to change into sleepwear in case they broke in. *How silly I am*, she thought. *If the Russians get in here, it won't make any difference to them what I am wearing. They will do as they please with me.*

She closed her eyes, trying to trust God, but she'd lost faith, and the ruckus in the streets made it impossible to rest. Every time she closed her eyes, a sound outside would jar her, and fear gripped her so hard that she felt her heart beat hard in her throat. The Russian soldiers might bust down the door at any moment, and then…?

Lotti sat up in bed and gathered the blanket around her. It was chilly outside, but she felt icy cold. Part of her wanted to run in panic, to leave Berni and hide in the subway with the others. But of course, she knew she never would. The guilt she would feel at leaving Berni in her weakened condition would be too hard for Lotti to live with.

As Lotti lay back down with the blanket tight around her body, alone on the bed, she began praying. At first, her prayers were words of anger, and her face was filled with tears of fury. But then, like a miracle, out of nowhere came an answer. Perhaps it was God? She wasn't sure, but it was crystal clear, an idea that flickered like a light in her brain.

Once in what seemed like a lifetime ago, when things were far better than they were, Alina, her best friend's daughter, had given her a tube of red lipstick as a gift. It was a joke at the time. Alina always told Lotti that she looked like an American movie star. All she needed was the cherry red lipstick. They'd both laughed. Then, when Lotti got Alina the job at the orphanage, Alina gave her lipstick as a gift. She'd only worn it a few times and saved it for special occasions. She was glad she had it because it might save Berni's and her lives.

It was nearly midnight, and the cries of anguish from the victims and the yelps of triumph from the victors continued in the streets below. Lotti's plans for the lipstick were still rolling around in her mind when she heard a loud, distressed female voice coming from outside the building: "The Soviet flag has been raised over the Reichstag."

It was time to act and act quickly. What was she waiting for? Her legs were wobbly with fear, but she got out of bed and took the lipstick from the bottom drawer on her nightstand. The tube felt cold in her hand as she swallowed hard, praying the lipstick had not dried up. She opened it. Testing it on the back of her hand, she saw that it was still in working condition. Quickly, she wiped the lipstick off her hand with a towel and went to Berni's bedside. Her hands were shaking as she began carefully dotting Berni's face, arms, and hands with the red lipstick so she would appear to have a severe rash. Once she'd finished, she took a moment to look at her work. It was convincing. But before she could draw the dots on herself, there was a pounding on the door.

"Open up," a harsh and determined male voice said. He was speaking in Russian. Lotti understood him because her late and beloved husband, Lev, had been a Russian Jew. Over the years that they were together, she became fluent in the language. *Oh my God, they're here. The Russians are here.*

He knocked again. Louder this time. She pulled the blanket tighter around her shoulders. Lotti felt sure he would break it down if she didn't open the door. If only she'd acted faster with the lipstick, but now it was too late.

Her hand shook as she opened the door.

"What the hell took you so damn long?" a tall young Russian soldier said, more of a statement than a question.

Lotti didn't answer.

Then she heard a stampede of boots on the stairs, and she knew he wasn't alone. A mob of wild, drunken Russians flooded into the small apartment. *Help me, Lev*, she whispered in her mind. *I am so afraid.*

One of the soldiers tore the blanket off Lotti. Then, he ripped her nightgown open and revealed her breasts. Instinctively, she grabbed the fabric to hide her modesty. All the soldiers roared with laughter. If only she'd had a few more minutes, she could have put the lipstick on herself like she had put on Berni. *Damn it.*

"There is another one sleeping in here," a soldier called out to his comrades. "This is going to be a good night for us." They were speaking in Russian. They thought Lotti didn't understand them, but she did. She could feel the fear rising within her. *At least Berni is heavily drugged, and with God's help, she'll sleep through this.*

"Wait," Lotti said, her voice cracking as she found the courage to speak. "My friend in that bedroom is very sick. She has a contagious disease. I realize you can do as you like with us, but be forewarned. I, too, have been exposed to the disease. It might be a day or two before I come down with the rash. But, just know you may catch what we have if you touch us."

The soldiers looked at each other. One of them went into the room where Bernadette lay, followed by the others and Lotti. He lit a match.

The lipstick dots looked like a red, vivid, and terrible rash in the light of the small flame.

"I've been taking care of her," Lotti warned. "She is my sister. I couldn't leave her, but I know that it is contagious."

"Let's get out of here," one of the soldiers said. "It does look terrible. And I sure as hell don't want to catch it."

"What about the other one. The healthy one?" another soldier asked, indicating Lotti.

"I want to get out of this apartment as soon as possible. There are women all over Berlin. Who needs this one. Did you see that stuff all over her? There's a disease in here, and I don't want it. What if it's true and the other one is carrying it? These women are not worth getting sick over. Just look outside all around you. There are plenty of other German women with whom to take our pleasure. Let's go."

"You're right. What the hell."

And just like that, they left the apartment, leaving the door ajar. With trembling hands and wobbly legs, Lotti walked over to the door and shut it, locking it. Then she fell to her knees and wept. The fake rash had worked this time. But there was no telling what would happen in the future. Thank God she still had some Pervitin. She'd gotten the amphetamine from her physician so she could stay awake when she worked all night. Then, she'd used it to keep her wits about her during the bombings.

Tonight, she would take it to stay awake, just in case more soldiers tried to come in. She dotted her own face and hands. This time, if they came, she would look sick, too. Then she lay awake trembling on her bed.

Still, Lotti knew it was only a matter of time before she would have to leave the apartment to get food and water if they were to survive.

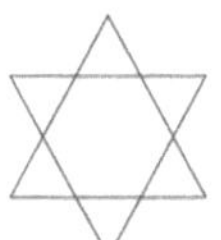

three

Lotti

NEARLY A WEEK HAD PASSED since the Russians came into Berlin. There was nothing to eat in the apartment, nothing left at all, and no one to ask for help. The women still living in the building didn't have any food either, and if they did, most of them would not have shared it with Lotti. Lotti knew she had no choice but to venture into the conquered city's dangerous streets to find food.

She glanced over at Berni, who was still asleep. Berni was doing much better. She was able to sit up in bed. With Lotti's help, Berni began to take short walks around the apartment. She was still weak, and there was no doubt that she needed food. But then, so did Lotti.

When Lotti gazed outside her apartment window, it looked like a macabre horror show of strange characters; all of them seemed unreal. There were dead bodies in the streets—some murdered, some sick from disease or starvation. There were the walking dead, people who had been reduced to skeletons, barely alive. Some had probably been hiding, others in the resistance.

Then, of course, there were those who had come out of the camps, their skin gray, their bodies broken, their eyes sunken in with the horrors they'd seen, still wearing the gray-striped uniforms. They walked the streets aimlessly, leaving notes on tree trunks, hoping to find lost family members.

Women who had dared to resist the sexual advances of Russian soldiers lay dead and mutilated, many of them naked and exposed in vulgar and horrifying positions. German deserters hung limp and rotting like scarecrows from poles.

And then, there were the Russian soldiers who walked through the streets like conquering gods. She couldn't help but think about Lev as she watched the concentration camp survivors stumbling along. If the Nazis hadn't killed her husband, he would be one of the broken and starved people she saw everywhere, but he would be on his way home to her. God, how she wished that Lev had been a survivor. Lotti would have given anything to have Lev back in her arms. She would have spent the rest of her life loving him back to life and to health.

Lev. Dear sweet Lev. He was older than she was, and wiser. So kind, so gentle, generous, and loving.

After Lev was gone, Lotti had given up on men entirely. She closed the book on love in her life forever, and although she was only thirty-seven now, she had not been touched by a man in many years.

To Lotti, being raped by one of these wanton savages was unthinkable. But even worse, if they assaulted Bernadette, the girl would surely die. Her body was only just recovering. Lotti doubted that Berni could withstand a brutal sexual attack.

Oh dear God, how could you have abandoned me this way? How could you have taken my Lev? Lev, oh God, Lev, I need your help. I am so scared. But then she bit her lower lip and opened Lev's closet.

This was the first time she'd looked at Lev's things since his death. His clothing hung neatly, just the way he'd left it. "Lev," Lotti whispered, burying her face in his shirt, trying to inhale a whiff of his essence. Tears stung the back of her eyes. "Lev, a day doesn't go by that I don't miss you,"

Then she bent down and touched his black shoes. Her mind drifted back to the days when they were first married. In the morning, she would lie, her head propped up on her pillow, watching him get dressed for work. He'd always sat at the edge of the bed when he put his shoes on, and after he was done, he'd walk over and kiss her goodbye before he left to go to the shop. Some days, she would languish in bed for a few minutes, with her head on his pillow, thinking about their lovemaking the night before. Her throat closed; the pain of remembering the past was too overwhelming. *This is not the time for sentimentality. Don't think. Don't think. Just act, or Berni will be dead by nightfall. And you won't be long after.*

She took one of Lev's shirts off the hanger. It was a white cotton work shirt, one he'd worn often. Lotti couldn't help but hold it against her cheek before she put it on. A tear slid onto the floor, but she ignored it. Then she took a pair of folded black pants and stepped into them. They were too big, so she tightened the belt. Well, most of Germany was starving. It wouldn't look strange to anyone to see a man walking down the street wearing clothing too big for him.

She rolled her feet into a pair of Lev's socks and stuffed the front of his shoes with old rags so that they would stay on her small, slender feet. Then she looked in the mirror. Her breasts and her hair were a dead giveaway. She tied a long scarf around her bosom, binding herself as tightly as possible. What other choice did she have?

When she was satisfied that her chest looked flat, she put the shirt back on. Now came the difficult part. Her hair had to go. *Don't think, just cut,* she told herself. The scissors sliced through her long locks. Lev had loved her golden hair. However, it was no longer as lush and golden; it had thinned out and was sprinkled with gray. As the curls fell to the ground, her heart sank. But there was no time to be sentimental. It must be done.

Short, shorter, until she looked like a man. The hair was cut unevenly. In some places, it was so short that her scalp was visible. She couldn't be sure how the Russians would respond to her if they thought she was a German man. She didn't want to risk their anger. So, she decided that she would claim to be a Jewish man who had been in hiding in the forest. Lotti knew that her clothes had to look worn and disheveled. She pulled a kitchen knife out of the drawer and tore holes in the garments. Then she took dirt from a flowerpot that had once held a plant, now dead, and smeared it on her face, clothes, and hands.

Then she found one of Lev's old hats, punched the top out, and placed it on her head. *We need food; we need water. I have to do this. I can't give in to fear. If we are to survive, I must leave this apartment.* Next, Lotti took what little cash she had and quietly said a prayer to God she was still angry with and one to Lev. Then she left the apartment.

four

Lotti

RUSSIAN UNIFORMS WERE EVERYWHERE she looked. They were like colonies of insects congregating outside of taverns and buildings. The conquerors were certainly proud of the power they held over the women of the city as they sauntered through the streets loud and laughing.

Empty glass vodka bottles lay shattered on the pavement.

Lotti felt her heart beating in her temples, and for a moment, she thought about running back to the apartment, but she forced herself to go forward. Picking up speed in her walk, Lotti passed an alleyway where a woman had been pushed up against a building. Her dress was torn, and she was naked from the waist down.

"Bitte. No…" The woman was crying softly, but the Russian soldier was not listening. He was pushing himself against her, and Lotti knew that the woman was being raped. *Faster*, she told herself. *Faster, or that woman could be you.* She was almost running now. Then Lotti turned a corner and saw a man in a German uniform lying on the ground, his face a mass of blood. He was being beaten with clubs and kicked by four Russian soldiers. His screams filled the streets. *Don't look. Don't turn your head. Keep your eyes forward, and keep moving, for God's sake.*

But just as she was about to enter a bakery, a Russian soldier wobbled over to her.

"You want some water or food?" he said.

What do I say? If he hears my voice, he'll know I'm a woman. She shook her head no.

"You don't need food and water? I think you do, and I think you are not a man…" he said, his eyebrow lifting as if he'd discovered a child playing hide and seek. A wicked smile came over his face, and Lotti felt like she might vomit.

A lump formed in her throat. He knew. He was probably going to rape her. She felt a phantom pain inside her womb. *Please, God, you have to help me. Please, not this.*

He pulled her into his arms. "You know, a woman looks very sexy in a man's clothes," he said. Lotti wondered if he was just talking to himself or if he somehow knew that she could understand him. "To dress as a man was a spunky idea. I like that. I like a woman who is clever and has a little fire."

She didn't smell alcohol on his breath. But she remembered Lev once telling her that vodka had no smell, and this man was stumbling like a drunk. Perhaps he was too drunk to overpower her. Lotti pushed him out of the way and started to run. He gave chase but tripped over a bump on the sidewalk and fell. She was still running when she ran right into the arms of another Russian soldier. He caught her, and when she looked up into his deep blue eyes, a pang of terror ripped through her heart.

Her hat had fallen off. Her freshly chopped hair stood up in tufts.

"What's going on here?" the man said.

She shook her head. "Let me go, please, let me go."

The man laughed. "I wasn't capturing you. I was just trying to keep you from falling," he said, letting her go. "Are you all right?"

"No," she said. "I'm not. That man is chasing me." She turned around to see the drunken soldier lying on the ground.

"Well, you seem to be safe now," the Russian said.

"I am not. I am not safe at all." Lotti was shaking. She was afraid she was going to cry.

"That's probably true," he said. "Where are you headed?"

She had no choice but to tell him. After all, he could rape her right now if he wanted to. Why not try to make him pity her? "My friend is very sick. She needs a doctor. If she doesn't get help, I think she might die. The streets are a terrifying place to be. Women are being raped and killed. Please don't hurt me or force me..."

"You don't have to worry about that. I don't need to force women to come to my bed. Plenty come willingly. And if it's not their choice, that takes the fun out of it, you know? So, pull yourself together, and I'll walk you to the doctor's office."

"But that man?" Lotti pointed to the man who lay on the ground.

"He won't bother you. It'll take him at least a day to sleep that drunken stupor off. Come on, let's go."

She walked beside him and realized that he was tall and strong. Lotti couldn't say that she liked him. But then again, he didn't have to be a gentleman. From what she could see happening on the streets, few were. Maybe she could ask him how she might get some food. She'd been lucky to find this man. Very lucky.

five
Alina

New York
May 1945

ALINA, the girl who had always been so shy, and tried to be so proper when she was young, now ran a whorehouse. As a child, Alina believed she would get married and have children, and her biggest dream was to study and become a teacher. But life had sent her in another direction, and she'd done what was necessary to survive.

In a way, she was proud of herself for being strong enough to go forward with her business despite losing the man she loved and the respect of society.

In the months since Alina had opened the business, she had gotten quite an education about how men behaved when they didn't need to pretend to be gentlemen. She'd seen men at their best. Some were strong and heroic by nature, but she'd also seen the male of the species at their worst. And at their worst, some were vile. But she never lost sight of why she'd opened this business. She needed money, plenty of money to ensure a safe future for her son. And, no matter the difficulties she must face, she would persevere. Joey must never be left to die because she lacked the funds for his proper medical care.

Every day, she was discovering more about running this tough business. Alina learned that alcohol had different effects on various types of men. Some grew quiet and complacent, others grew needy. The ones who became violent were of the greatest concern. There were fights at least three times a week, and occasionally, one of the girls was beaten.

Alina knew she had to do something. From what her employees told her, the customers were more unruly at her brothel than they were when they frequented whorehouses owned by men. She realized she needed men with physical strength to keep the customers in line.

One afternoon, Alina asked one of the girls to tell Klara to come into Alina's office. So that they could speak alone, she sent Joey to the kitchen to ask the cook to prepare him a snack.

Klara knocked on the door.

"Come in. Sit down. I need some advice," Alina said, sitting behind her desk.

"Of course." Klara sat down.

"As you know, the patrons don't respect me. They think that because I am a woman, they can do as they please when they are here at the house. I have to hire some men to keep these fellows in line. Strong men. But, we have to be sure that they will not be averse to having a female boss. You know a lot of people. Do you have any ideas?"

"I know two men who would be good candidates. They worked for the house I worked for when I first came here."

"Do you think they are still working there?" Alina asked. "It's bad enough that we stole the girls from another brothel owner. Now, we would be taking someone's bouncers as well."

"That's business." Klara shrugged. Then she smiled. "I'll find out what they are getting paid. Offer them more. They'll be happy to change jobs."

"Klara. Have you no scruples?"

"None." Klara laughed.

"You are a terrible person. But you are such a wonderful friend, and as bad as you are, I love you. You've become like a sister to me."

"Don't worry about a thing. I'll take care of it."

"Thank you…"

"By the way, their names are Sid and Earl. You'll like them."

Three days later, Sid and Earl came to work for Alina. As Klara promised, both men were very respectful of Alina and the other employees. They treated Alina not as a man or woman but as a boss. The new security guards were polite and considerate to the girls.

Klara found out what they earned, and then she and Alina decided on an amount to pay them. Sid and Earl had almost doubled their salary, and they returned the favor by keeping the male clients under control. Alina also hired a piano player, a good-natured, dark-skinned man of an undetermined age, who called himself Cool Breeze. His smooth voice and skill with the jazz piano were unmatchable. His witty remarks and entertaining stories with underlying life lessons earned him the affectionate nickname "the philosopher." Alina paid him well. Money was plentiful. And because she was secure, she wanted to be fair and make sure her employees were happy and comfortable.

The girls who worked for her loved Alina. Unlike other houses, they had the option to refuse a client if they desired. They rarely did, but just knowing they had the choice made the working environment calm and easy. The girls were paid better here than anywhere else in the city. The food and the accommodations were better, too.

Alina was a reasonable boss, but the girls learned quickly that she was certainly no pushover. She demanded that her employees keep themselves clean and attractive. They were not permitted to drink while they lived in the house, and cursing was not tolerated. Although it was a brothel, and Alina never deluded herself into thinking it was a decent business, she would keep it as respectable as possible under the circumstances.

Joey was growing up, and even though he was living in a brothel, he had the benefit of his mother being around all the time. Not only did he have Alina, but he also had the comfort and attention of twelve surrogate mothers. Since he was the only child living in the house, all the girls pampered him. They were careful to keep him as ignorant of what was happening in the house as possible.

Alina put him to bed early, and he was not to leave his room once night fell. Joey's room was adjacent to Alina's, and it had a bathroom. There was plenty of space for his toys and no need for him to go downstairs once the customers arrived. Still, Alina sometimes felt guilty about bringing her son up in a house of ill repute. But she couldn't help but feel affection towards her employees when she saw how much the girls adored him. His little broken body endeared him to the women. They'd been hardened by seeing men at their lowest, but this harmless, quiet little boy with the twisted legs brought out maternal instincts many of the girls didn't know they had.

The house had a good reputation, and so due to word of mouth, the clientele was growing rapidly. Each month, the profits were higher than the last. Alina couldn't have asked for more, and she was pleased that she'd chosen to open the business, but was terribly lonely.

Things were going just as she'd planned. She would have the material wealth she had hoped for, and Joey would have whatever he needed as he got older. But in turn, she knew that because her family would be ashamed of her lifestyle, she must never return to Germany and search for them. It had been years since she'd seen her parents, sister, and best friend, Lotti. Although she promised herself she would never see Ugo again, she was worried sick about him. He could be dead already, and she would never even know that he'd been killed in battle. Because she wasn't his wife, no one would come to inform her.

Spring was cool in New York, and the air was crisp and breezy. The windows were open in the brothel. All the male clientele from the night before were already gone. Joey was playing a game on the floor with one of the girls. Alina sat down at the kitchen table and called for Maybelline, the woman who kept the house clean and did the cooking.

"Yes, ma'am. Would you like some breakfast?"

There had been an incident the previous night. Things had been going along as usual until a new customer arrived. He was a tall, handsome man, far too handsome to be paying for the company of a lady.

Alina was angry with herself for not realizing this. She should have seen the problems before they escalated. But she didn't.

The customer had been allowed to go to a room with one of her girls. And it was only when they'd heard the screaming downstairs that Alina realized why the customer had needed to come to a brothel. By the time Sid got to the room, the girl had a broken nose and had to be sent to the hospital. Then things got even worse when the customer refused to leave without a fight. Sid hit him, and then he tried to return the blow. Sid knocked him to the ground and threw him out the door. Some of the knickknacks in the house were broken, and glass was everywhere. During the squabble, one of the girls had been pushed against a china cabinet. Her arm had needed five stitches.

Because of the bouncers, this sort of thing didn't happen often. But when it did, Alina was unnerved. It was a harsh reminder that she owned a shady business where anything could happen.

"Ma'am? Breakfast?" Maybelline asked again.

"Oh, I'm sorry for not answering. My mind was wandering. Breakfast? No, thank you, May. I'm not hungry. Just a cup of coffee would be wonderful," Alina said.

"Black with sugar like always?"

"Yes. Thank you."

Alina lit a cigarette. Most of the girls smoked. And lately, she, too, had begun smoking. It calmed her nerves.

"Has anyone seen Meredith this morning? Poor thing. I can't believe her nose is broken," Alina said.

"She's all right. I checked on her when I got up. I'm sure she's probably still hurting," one of the girls answered as she was stirring her coffee with slender fingers adorned with strawberry nail polish.

"And Joan. I think she had to have five stitches."

"She was fine last night. I haven't seen her since. She's still upstairs sleeping."

Alina pulled her silk robe tighter around her slender waist and retied the belt. She sipped her coffee and looked out the window. Even though she felt guilty about the two girls who had gotten hurt, she couldn't be sorry that she'd decided to open the house. The money was flowing.

But damn if she didn't wish Ugo had been less stubborn about her business. They could have been financially comfortable. Damn him, if only she could have convinced him that he would earn more money working with her than he ever could delivering furniture. They could have done this together.

But, of course, Alina would never have asked Ugo to be a partner in a business like this. He wasn't that kind of man. Although she hated the fact that he was so stubborn, at the same time, she knew that his character and integrity were some of the most pressing reasons why she loved him.

Alina inhaled deeply from her cigarette. If only she could just talk to him now. She needed a friend, and even though she had Klara, it would be good to have a partner, someone to share her life. There was something special about Ugo. Alina always felt she could trust him. She took a sip of coffee. It was getting cold. She put the cup back on the saucer, and her thoughts returned to Ugo. It would be nice to hear his voice. *Stop thinking about him. He's gone. Everyone in Germany is gone. No point in dwelling on the past. From now on, it's just Joey and me.* And, of course, Klara.

Joey came limping out of the living room. He was all she had left. Her small, underweight son with his slender, twisted legs. She loved that child with a love she never knew she could feel. He needed her in a way no one in her life had ever needed her.

"Mama, I drew this for you," he said, handing her a picture of a bird.

"Joey, it's lovely," Alina said, and it was.

Klara came into the dining room. Her fiery red hair was set in curlers, and she had a thick layer of white, pasty cream on her face. Alina was amazed that Klara had turned out to be her dearest friend. How strange, considering she was Ugo's ex-wife. Real friends turned up in the oddest of places.

"Rough night last night," Klara said. "May I?" She pointed to the cigarette package in front of Alina. "I am all out."

"Sure, of course, help yourself."

"The business can be like that sometimes," Klara said.

"You mean rough customers?"

"Yes, I've learned that men have all kinds of reasons for going to a whore. Some are lonely and need affection. They're usually old, widowers, or shy and unattractive. Others are unhappy sexually with their wives. They have important jobs and need a girl who will be discreet. And then there are those that are just sexually perverse. It takes getting used to."

Alina nodded. "Yes, I suppose it does." It was odd how close she and Klara had grown over the last few months. When she'd first met Klara, Alina had been jealous. After all, Klara had a connection to Ugo. But once the business opened, and Klara proved to be the most valuable friend Alina could imagine, she'd started to really like Klara.

Klara was funny, sincere, and really smart. At first, it was difficult for Alina to talk about Ugo with Klara. But Klara was so matter-of-fact about the breakup with her husband that it became easier for them to discuss him.

"Ugo would have been shocked at how strong and capable you were last night," Klara said, taking a bite of a buttered biscuit. "Mmm, that's good," she added, closing her eyes and savoring the flavor of the hot, doughy bread.

Alina's face turned red. "Why do you say that about Ugo, I mean?"

"Because when he used to come and see our daughter, God rest her soul, he would talk about you sometimes. He thought you were such a delicate flower." She laughed. "You're tough as nails, Alina. That's why I like you."

"You're teasing me," Alina said, shaking her head.

"No, just telling you the truth. Ugo is in love with you, you know that, don't you?"

"I am not sure that I believe it. To tell you the truth, Klara, I'm not sure I believe in love. But what surprises me is that you knew he had feelings for me all along, and it didn't bother you?" Alina asked.

"Yes, I knew, and no, it never bothered me. From working in this profession, I've become an expert on men. I was never jealous because

I knew Ugo and I had no future together. We were sweethearts in a different land, a different time and place. Once I got here to America, I knew he and I wouldn't see eye to eye. We just don't share the same goals or dreams.

He wants a wife and children. He's satisfied being mediocre, a working man, living a simple life. Ugo doesn't have aspirations for greatness. I do. I want a man with more money than I know what to do with. I grew up poor in Russia, very poor. I lived on a farm where we got up before sunrise and worked in the fields all day just to have enough food to survive. In the winter, it was freezing cold. Starvation, disease, and early death were a way of life for us. My parents had eight children. Three of us survived to adulthood. The first two died before they were a year old. That was our way of life. So, when I came to America, I was determined to find gold on the streets, as they say." She laughed. "And I am going to find it, maybe not on the streets, but in my bed, and when I do, I am going to marry it."

"So you have been telling me the truth all along. You really aren't in love with Ugo."

"I love him, but more like an old friend from the past than a lover. We were just children when we met. I was a teenager, he was handsome, and I was infatuated, you know? But Ugo is one of those straight-laced fellas who would rather live by the book than earn a lot of money. I want a man who is living the American dream. I'm tired of hard work. Ugo is just not that man. He is so proud that even though he loves you, he can't cope with the fact that you own this house. This is a big problem for him. He's always been far too prideful and so moral. It's pitiful and really sad that he is willing to let you go for such a stupid reason. But I know him, and I'll tell you this, the damn fool is in love with you. He just wants you to marry him and be satisfied with whatever he is able to give you. He has a strong sense of what he feels is right and wrong. In a way, this is what makes Ugo a noble kind of guy, but it's also what keeps him from true happiness."

"Aren't most men like that? I mean, how many men do you know that would be comfortable with their wives owning a brothel?"

"None." Klara laughed. "But you're a different breed than the average woman. You don't care what people say about you as long as you have what you need. That's why I like you. You give men the impression that you are weak and helpless. They like that. It makes them feel powerful and needed. But the truth is, Alina, you're stronger than most. You may not want to hear this, but I know you care for Ugo, too. In many ways, the two of you are a lot alike. You have your own mind. I am not saying there is anything wrong with it, but you are not willing to sacrifice your independence for love."

"I can't. It's for Joey that I'm doing this."

"And for yourself, too. As long as you have your own money, you don't have to ever put up with a bastard like Trevor again."

Alina and Klara had talked about Trevor extensively since they'd become friends. "Yes, that's true. I learned a lot from marrying him. I learned that when you don't have your own money, you don't have any control over your life."

"Yes, but I'll tell you a secret if you want to know."

"That's up to you," Alina sipped her coffee. She was curious, especially if what Klara had to tell her was about Ugo.

"I have money saved, and I don't plan to be a whore forever. You know Marcus, my client, the attorney? The successful one? I am trying to find a way to convince him to marry me. I've been trying to get pregnant by him, but so far, no luck."

"He's an old man," Alina said. "You want him to marry you? I'm surprised he can still have sex."

"Most of the time, he can't. That's the problem. If he was more able, I'd be pregnant already. He only comes to see me so he can prove to himself that he is still sexually desirable. It's a private little game we play." Klara winked. "He might be an old man, but he is a rich old man. And old men have a short life span," Klara said, then she laughed.

Alina shook her head. "Klara, you're quite the character." Alina laughed, too.

Klara lit a cigarette and took Alina's hand. "Listen, there is something that I have to talk to you about. It's serious."

Alina took a cigarette out of the pack and lit it, then put an ashtray between her and Klara. "Can we talk here, or should we go into my room where we can talk privately."

"No, here is fine. I just want to let you know that Trevor has found you. He came by the house looking for you yesterday. He knows where you and Joey are living. A man like that is dangerous, Alina."

"If he does anything, I'll have him arrested," Alina said. The sweat beaded at her temple. *Oh my God. Why couldn't he just disappear? Trevor was here. He'd found me. He had stood right here in my house.* She looked at her hand. It was trembling. *Damn that dirty bastard. He still has the power to frighten me.*

"If he does anything, it will be too late to have him arrested."

"Right now, there is nothing I can do because he hasn't done anything to Joey or me," Alina said, taking a drag of her cigarette.

"That's what I figured," Klara said. "But I wanted you to know and keep your eyes open. I don't trust him."

"Yes, I will," Alina said. She was worried about Joey.

"Klara…"

"Yes?"

"Don't mention it to the girls. I don't want to start a panic. But between us. I'm terrified."

six

Lotti

OVER THE NEXT TWO MONTHS, Berlin slowly began to come alive again. Some of the restaurants and cabarets reopened. The subway and phones were up and running. An Aryan and a Jew were married legally!

This was the first marriage of its kind since the Nuremberg laws had been instated. For some people, especially Jews, it brought a glimmer of hope. The Russian soldiers were still frightening to the Germans, and they were in control.

Since they were the only source of food for the German women, the Russian soldiers thought they were sexually entitled to use the woman at will. If she could have, Lotti would have stayed inside her apartment forever. It was not a guarantee of safety because the soldiers were coming into the women's homes. However, it was still safer than the streets.

Still, Lotti had to venture out to go back to work and to find food, water, and firewood. Berni was getting back to herself. She could get out of bed and walk around the apartment, but Lotti was still worried when she left Berni alone.

One evening, when she and Berni had just finished dinner, Lotti took Berni's hand and led her into the bedroom where Lotti slept. She opened the drawer to the nightstand.

"I have a gun. You see? It's loaded. In case something happens when I am not at home, I want you to know where it is."

Berni's eyes grew wide. "I have never fired a gun."

"Me either. But it's here. I suppose you just pull the trigger," Lotti said as she lifted the firearm with a trembling hand. "I don't know if I'd have the nerve to use it. In fact, I'd almost be afraid that the intruder might take it away and use it on us," Lotti said.

"I wouldn't be afraid to use it. If a man came in here threatening us, I'd kill him. I have no doubt about that," Berni said. Her eyes were hard like glass. "Give it to me. Let me see it."

Carefully, Lotti handed the gun to Berni. "I think I know how to use it. I remember my father had a gun. He shot rabbits and small animals. It made me sick. But I think I remember how it works," Berni said, turning the gun over. "Yes. I think I remember." She returned the weapon to Lotti, who put it safely in the drawer.

One afternoon, Berni was inside the house, and Lotti was on her way to the water pump to replenish their supply when Lotti was attacked by two Russian soldiers in the alleyway of their building.

This time, Lotti was not as fortunate as she had been in the past. This time, she could not escape. Two men forced themselves on her, taking turns. One held her down, the other raped her. It took less than a half hour, but it felt like a lifetime in hell.

They didn't hit, punch, or kick her. They weren't exceptionally brutal with their thrusts. But then again, Lotti didn't fight. She went limp like a rag doll, far too terrified to fight. She was in shock, unable to cry or even to move.

Neither of the men even spoke. They just grunted. When they were done, they left her sitting on the gravel. Lotti was shaking uncontrollably. She was stunned, still unable to cry. Her body felt invaded. It was like a stranger to her, a stranger she hated. Her breath was shallow, and as much as she wanted to lie down on the pavement and die, she knew instinctively that it was too dangerous to stay in the alley.

More Russians might come at any minute. Then, she would have to endure the same thing again. It was best to get up and try to get to the water fountain. Her legs were weak and wobbly as she pulled on her underwear and straightened her dress. Then Lotti began to walk quickly towards the fountain.

"Oh God, Lev. Oh God. What am I going to do? This could happen again at any time," she whispered to the empty sidewalk. Holding on to the wall of the building, she forced herself to hurry along until she felt bile rise in her throat. Nausea overcame her, forcing her to stop and vomit the contents of her empty stomach. No one on the street paid her any attention as she retched.

She finally got to the fountain. There was a line. There was always a line. When she got to the front, she pumped the water until her bucket was full, noticing that there was still some vomit on her hand. She poured some water over it and washed it off. Then, quickly, she made her way back to the apartment.

After Lotti put the water away, she checked on Berni, who had fallen asleep. A pang of resentment towards Berni came over Lotti. Now, she had to go back out and see if she could find some food. She'd enjoyed caring for others all her life, but right now, she needed some help, and there was no one to depend on but herself.

On her way to a shop she hoped would be open, Lotti saw a group of women, Trümmerfrau, cleaning up the street and clearning up pieces of rubble. She wanted to keep going but felt she must help, at least for a while.

After an hour, she left and went on her way, looking for bread. Most of the bakeries were closed. They had trouble finding the ingredients and fuel to run their ovens. Lotti walked for several miles before finding an open bakery where she could buy a single loaf. With bread in hand, she began to rush back towards home. She wanted to be off the street before nightfall.

When Lotti walked into the apartment, Berni stood up.

"My God, Lotti, what happened to you?"

"I was helping a group of Trümmerfrau to clean the streets."

"You're a mess. Your dress is covered with blood."

"I cut my hand," Lotti said.

It was true. Berni cleaned the cut and bandaged it. "I'm ready to go out and start helping. I'm doing much better now," Berni said.

"You can't." Lotti shook her head, feeling guilty for her resentment towards Berni earlier that day. Berni had been through a lot. She was still weak. Lotti didn't want her to get hurt.

"If you can do it, I can too," Berni said.

"No."

"Why?"

"Sit down, Berni," Lotti said, taking Berni's hand and leading her to the sofa. "Something happened to me today. It's been happening a lot to the women here in Berlin. I was raped by two soldiers, Berni. After your recent hospitalization, something like that might kill you. And, well, it's very probable that this will happen to you if you go out on the street."

Berni's face froze into a mask, white and pale like plaster. She didn't speak, but she was grinding her teeth.

"Berni, listen to me. You have to keep yourself together," Lotti said.

"I hate men," Berni growled like a wounded animal.

Lotti had never seen Berni look like this. Berni's eyes had turned to glass, unseeing. Her teeth were bared.

"I hate them all," Berni said, and she swallowed hard. Then, in an instant, her face crumpled, and she began to weep into her fists. "My stepfather raped me for years. From the time I was ten years old."

"I'm so sorry," Lotti said.

"He told me that if I told my mother, he would kill me. I finally told her. I had to. I couldn't take it anymore. I would rather have died. And you know what she said? She took his side. She didn't believe me." Berni wiped her nose on her sleeve. "The baby… the baby I aborted… It was his baby. He raped me, and I got pregnant. Then I ran away."

"Oh," Lotti said. She touched Berni's arm, but Berni pulled back.

"The next time a man tries to touch me against my will, I will kill him. I swear it. I'll take a knife and plunge it through his rotting heart."

Lotti couldn't speak. She saw the pain in Berni's face, so she took Berni into her arms and rocked her like a child. Terror and shock from what happened to her that day still hung over Lotti like a dark cloud. But she'd always put others first, and even though she was in pain, she hid it. Instead, she did what Lotti always did. She tried to comfort someone else who was in need.

That night, after Berni fell asleep, Lotti lay awake in bed. It had been a horrific day. She was still in pain, not only because she'd been brutally violated, but also because she'd scrubbed her female parts raw, trying to remove the residue that the Russians had left behind.

Oh God, how are we ever going to get through this? Are we to live in terror forever from now on? The Russians are here to stay. A single tear fell on her pillow.

Well, at least she finally understood why Berni had gone for the abortion.

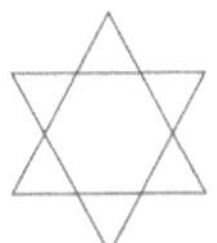

seven

Alina

New York
June 1945

ALINA WENT into town on a beautiful Saturday afternoon. There was a slight breeze that spring morning, and she felt light in her step.

There were cigarette burns on the sofa, and Maybelline had offered to reupholster it if she got the fabric. There was a lovely fabric store right outside of Chinatown, and the prices were reasonable. So, she'd taken a streetcar and was going through bolts of fabric, trying to decide which would work best in the living room.

The hair stood on her neck as she felt someone's hot breath steaming behind her. She tried to turn to see who was standing so close to her. But as she moved, her assailant moved as well, and she could not see his face.

Then, quietly but threateningly, Trevor whispered in Alina's ear. "You're embarrassing me all over this town. I won't have it. How dare you leave me the way you did. You stole money from me, too. I can't prove it, but I know it. And make no mistake, Alina, I am not a man to be toyed with. I will hurt you more than you've ever been hurt before. For the rest of your life, you'd better be looking behind you because you just won't know when I am going to strike. But, believe me, I will strike, and you will be sorry for this. Very sorry." He didn't touch her, yet Alina could feel the heavy heat of his body against hers.

"Are you threatening me, Trevor?" she asked. But when she turned to look at him, he was gone. His words unnerved her. She was shaking. Her mouth was dry. How was she going to get away from him?

eight
Alina

IT WAS late afternoon before Alina returned to the house. The day had started so beautifully, but now, the sun was overshadowed by a cluster of soft gray clouds, and a light drizzle began to fall. Alina put her handbag on the living room sofa and dropped down beside it. Klara came in from the kitchen.

"Did you buy some fabric?" Klara asked.

"No." Alina shook her head. She was spent.

"Mommy!" Joey said as he limped into her arms. Alina lifted her son onto her lap. He was so light, so weightless, that it frightened her.

"You look pale, what is it?" Klara sat down on the sofa next to Alina. "Are you feeling alright? Do you want me to get you some water?"

"No, I am fine," Alina said.

"You're not fine," Klara said, getting up. "Come, Joey." She lifted him into her arms. "You go to your room and play. Your mama and I need to talk." Klara turned to Alina. "Let me get him settled in his room, and I'll be right back."

Alina nodded. "I'll see you in a little bit, Joey? Alright."

"Yes, Mama."

He was such a good child, and because he was, his physical weakness was even more painful to Alina. She was still unnerved. The meeting with Trevor had shaken her to the very core. Now, she felt like she might never leave the house again, and even worse, she was terrified to let Joey out of her sight for even a minute.

It was almost like a prison she'd created in her mind. Trevor had hurt her before; what would keep him from doing it again? And he knew that Joey was her heart. If he wanted to destroy her, he would hurt Joey. That was her greatest fear. She would rather die than see Joey hurt.

Klara came down the stairs. "I went out to buy food today. You remember that you gave the cook the day off?"

"I forgot," Alina said.

"It's alright. I knew you would forget so I went shopping. Come sit in the kitchen while I put the food away. We should talk. You look terrible," Klara said.

Alina followed Klara and sat down at a chair by the work table. She lit a cigarette and watched as Klara opened the door to the icebox. The block of ice was in place. The ice man had made his delivery today. Klara put the perishables, the milk, the cheese, and the chicken inside. The bread would be fine on the counter.

"I bought chicken. I am going to try to fry it," Klara said, "for dinner tonight."

Alina smiled. "I'm sure May will be jealous of your cooking."

Klara laughed. "I'm not as good as May, but I'll try." Klara dried her hands on a dish towel and sat down beside Alina. "Alright, now tell me what's going on with you."

"I saw Trevor today. I was in the fabric store. He snuck up on me. He threatened me. I am scared for Joey, Klara."

"Yes, he is just the type of bastard who would do something to a child. We have to be very careful."

"I can't even allow the girls to take Joey to the park to play anymore. Trevor could do something to him. But how can I stop Joey from going outside? He has such a tough life as it is," Alina said, shaking her head. She took a long drag on her cigarette. The smoke filled her lungs and calmed her.

"I have to agree with you. You can't let Joey out of your sight. But you have to be careful, too."

"Yes, and I will. But more importantly, I'm going to have to have Sid and Earl keep an eye on Joey. I want him watched at all times. I don't care how much extra they want me to pay them. Joey's safety is worth it. I'll have one of them go along whenever one of the girls takes Joey to the park."

"I think that is a good idea."

Yes, Alina thought. *This is what I will do.* For now, it would give her some peace of mind. Not complete peace of mind, but at least some.

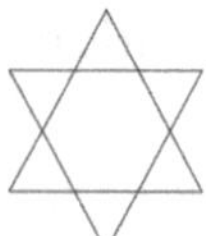

nine

WHEN THE NAZIS SURRENDERED, Germany was divided between the Allies: a sector went to France, another to Britain, one to the US, and then another to the Russians. Berlin, as the capital, was also to be divided.

It was a race to see which of these countries would set their flag in Berlin. Stalin made sure it was Russia, and before anyone else arrived, Russia planted roots in the broken city. As each of the Allies took its share, Russia still kept a stronghold and stood guard over her conquest.

And then, nine weeks after the fall of Berlin and the surrender of the Nazis, the Americans arrived.

ten
Lotti

Berlin
Summer 1945

LOTTI AND BERNI lived in a sector of Berlin known as Kreuzberg, in the American-run section of the city. The Americans weren't perfect by any means; they, too, were angry with the German women for the friends they'd lost in battle, but they were not nearly as brutal as the Russians.

Lotti had hope for the future for the first time in a long time. The food rations were still low, but she had gotten used to living that way. After all, the Germans had endured rationing since Goering had imposed it on them in 1939.

It was true that the Russians still policed the area, and their presence was always a part of her life, but Lotti's natural optimism began to emerge again. Life would never be joyous the way it had been when she was happily married to Lev, but it was getting brighter. The cinemas had opened, and so had the public pools. There was even a philharmonic concert in late May.

At the time, Berni was still too weak to attend, but it was a good sign that the people of Berlin were coming back to life. Lotti was relieved to see the return of some sense of normalcy. But, with the return of civilized living, she couldn't help but think about Lev. If only Lev had survived, she would have been happy, even with the rations and the threat of the Russians.

A few months earlier, she and Berni had been rounded up by a group of other German women in June. They had been bussed for twenty-two miles to Sachsenhausen, where they were forced to walk through a concentration camp to witness what the Nazis did to prisoners.

This was their punishment for being German, and it was a terrible day for Lotti. Lotti watched as so many of the women wept. How could the soldiers not know that not every German woman had agreed with Hitler? Many of them went along with the Third Reich out of fear for themselves or their families.

But for Lotti, this trip to the concentration camp was even more terrible. No one understood how personal all of this was for her. She'd never sanctioned the doctrine of the Third Reich, yet they considered her a part of all that had happened. And walking through that camp, all she could think of was her friends.

Had Michal, Alina, or even Taavi ended up in one of those places after he'd come to see her that last time? Had any of them survived? Were they murdered? Did their bodies lay in a pile somewhere like the bodies she now saw? These people who lay dead were once mothers, fathers, sisters, brothers, and friends.

Vomit rose in her throat. Dear God, how could anyone do this to a fellow human being? As she walked through the camps and saw the terrible conditions, the murderous gas chambers, and the heaps of skeletal dead bodies, she was glad in a strange way that if he wasn't to have survived, at least Lev had died quickly.

After the women left the confines of the camp, they were all silent as the bus that brought them rambled along for twenty-two miles back to Berlin, back to the safety of their homes. Lotti and Berni did not speak, but Lotti felt queasy as she whispered prayers for her lost friends. It was then that she decided she must begin looking for them as soon as possible. With God's help, Alina, Michal, or Taavi might still be alive. She'd already sent a letter to Gilde in Britain, but it had returned to her with no known address.

When Lotti thought about little Gilde, she felt guilty. Gilde had disappeared. Was she alive? Lotti had no idea. How could Lotti not feel guilty about Gilde? After all, she had been the one to convince Alina to send Gilde off with the Kindertransport. But with the bombings of London, it was hard to say whether Gilde had survived.

And how about her brother? Where was Johan? The last she'd seen him, he and Alina had moved in together in Munich. Then, without warning, both of them were gone. She'd never heard another word from either of them. Were they murdered, God forbid? Would she ever see either of them again?

On trees, on the sides of buildings, everywhere she looked, people had put up posts with the names of their missing family members or friends they were searching for. She would put up a post, too. Not that deep in her heart, she truly believed it would help, but it couldn't hurt. If she gave up hope, then there would be no reason to continue living.

eleven

Alina

New York
July 1945

ALINA'S WHOREHOUSE was a booming business, earning more money than she had ever dreamed possible. Alone in her room, she worked the numbers weekly and marveled at the money men were willing to spend for companionship.

It was slower during the week but full on the weekend. Even with so many of the younger men off fighting in the Pacific. The ones still in the States always found the money to pay for whores and liquor. Klara had told her this before she opened the whorehouse. Klara had said that even during the depression, when food was scarce, and jungle camps filled the parks, somehow men found a way to fulfill their carnal needs. She hadn't believed it then, but she had come to see it was true.

Sometimes, Alina worried about how growing up in a brothel would affect Joey, but everyone was kind to him. In fact, Alina had never seen a single person, client, employee, or prostitute treat him with anything but kindness.

However, Alina knew he also saw many things she wished he'd

never been exposed to. She tried to protect him, but it was impossible to shelter him completely. He was to stay in his room at night, but sometimes, he wandered downstairs for a glass of water or something to eat. Once evening fell, the women walked around the house scantily clad as the clients drifted in and made their nightly choices.

Joey never said a word about what he saw, but Alina wondered how much he knew and what he was thinking, watching all of it. Most of the time, she tried to stay up in her rooms with Joey, reading to him or telling him stories. But even as they lay on his bed, Alina reading him a bedtime story, they sometimes overheard vulgar language and loud laughter coming from downstairs or from one of the girl's rooms. There was no doubt in Alina's mind that her parents would never have approved.

Looking back, she remembered that her mother was not so innocent. She'd been young during the time when Taavi and Michal had separated. She'd never known why they broke up or what brought them back together. She'd been too young to understand at the time.

But she had hated Michal so many times, for so many things. She'd been so unforgiving and hard on her mother. She was angry when Michal took Otto as a lover. Then, she was angry when Michal's lover died, and Michal sent his sister to live with his family. Alina had become so close with Otto's sister, and then, just like the snap of a finger, Bridget, Otto's sister, was gone. And then again, Alina was angry when Michal brought Taavi back into their lives. That was at first, anyway.

Then Alina had come to truly adore her loving father. With all that Alina had done in her life to survive, she wished she could have one more chance to tell Michal that she understood how life's path could lead one in so many confusing directions.

When he grew up, what would Joey say about his childhood? Would Joey ever understand what she had done and why? Would he forgive her? She would tell him about his father when he was old enough to understand.

Someday, Alina would tell him how much Johan loved her and that they couldn't marry in Germany. The hard part would be to explain

Hitler and the cruelty of the Nuremberg laws that kept them apart. But she would explain when the time came. Then, she would tell Joey how she and his father planned to marry when they got to America. But things went bad when he died on the ship, leaving her alone to fend for herself.

She would explain to Joey how she had married Trevor, hoping he would take care of her and her child. But Trevor was a terrible, violent, and abusive man. That was when she knew she had to earn her own money. Alina would do her best to make her son understand how she'd tried to get work without success. So, she'd opened the brothel to make enough money to care for him and herself. Would she be able to make him understand? Well, it didn't matter right now because at least she could put a roof over his head and food on the table. And for now, to hell with anything else.

Trevor continued to do little things that would remind Alina that he was always watching. Sometimes, he left notes outside the front door that said, "I was thinking of you." Of course, he never signed them, but they stunk of his cologne, and she had no doubt who'd put them there. They were quiet threats. Not real enough to complain to the police, but real enough to keep her unnerved.

Sometimes, when things settled down in the wee hours of the morning, and Joey was still asleep, Alina was alone and awake, and she would sit at her dressing table watching the sunrise from her room. Those were the times when her mind would drift to thoughts of Ugo. He'd always been such a good friend. The very thought that he might be dead somewhere across the world was so horrible that it was unimaginable to her. And, yet, she knew that it was more than possible. The Japanese were not going to surrender. And every day, there were reports of more casualties.

News spread quickly in the house. Men talked to the girls about things they would never discuss outside the walls of the brothel. Alina had heard about internment camps where the Japanese Americans who had been forced from their homes had been sent to live since the war between Japan and America had begun. And from how the men who'd seen the camps described them, the conditions were deplorable.

Most of the girls were in agreement with the containment of the Japanese, but the very idea of it frightened Alina. Somehow, it seemed un-American to her, more like something the Nazis might do. Yet, she couldn't say that to anyone. So many of the clients had lost their sons in the war. Some had been killed in the bombing of Pearl Harbor. Hatred for the Japanese had become, in many ways, a sign of patriotism. Even though many Japanese had been born in America, their neighbors and friends looked at them differently. They were now the enemy because Japan attacked Pearl Harbor.

Then, in early August, one of the regular clients, Clifton Roberts, came in to see Amy, a girl he'd been keeping company with for several months. He was an older, educated man, a retired judge. Alina liked him. He was soft-spoken and never caused any trouble. So, when Clifton came in talking about America having bombed Japan with some sort of nuclear bomb, Alina listened. "It's all over the radio," Roberts said. "There was an inscription on the side of the bomb that said 'Greetings from the men of the Indianapolis.' It's a good thing that the Indianapolis wasn't in Pearl Harbor when the Japs bombed it, or it would have been lost too. This was one hell of a bomb. It was unlike anything we've ever seen before."

"Well, after what them Japs did at Pearl Harbor, they deserved what they got, alright," Judith, one of the girls, said. Then she lifted a bottle and poured Roberts a glass of wine.

"I agree with you. But you don't understand. This was a bomb like none before. It was mass destruction. Alina?"

"Yes, Judge Roberts?"

"Can you turn on the radio, please?"

"Of course." Alina turned the dial until the voices on the radio were clear.

"Listen to this," Roberts said, loud enough for everyone in the room to hear.

Since he'd always been such a quiet man, when he raised his voice, everyone listened. The crowd grew silent as the voice on the radio began to explain.

From what Alina could gather, President Truman had ordered that a plane called the Enola Gay drop this large nuclear bomb on Hiroshima to force the Japanese to surrender. The bomb was equal to the force released by 12,500 tons of TNT. It had caused mass destruction. Nuclear bomb? A bomb stronger and more destructive than any they'd ever known. Terrifying news. How would the Japanese retaliate?

Alina was afraid, and from the looks of the others in the room, she was sure they were also worried. *And what about Ugo? Dear God, where was Ugo during all of this?* She couldn't bear to think of what might have happened to him.

Still, even after the terrible destruction of Hiroshima, Japan still would not surrender.

For the next three days, Alina heard the bombing mentioned at least a dozen times. And then, three days later, over the radio came a news report that the United States had dropped a second bomb on the Japanese city of Nagasaki.

Again, mass death and destruction.

The following month, Japan surrendered.

twelve

Gilde

London
September 1945

EVERY NIGHT OF THE SHOW, following their performance, the actors came outside the back door to sign autographs for the fans. In her gold lamé gown, Gilde Thornbury opened the backstage door and walked outside with pen in hand to the music of loud applause. She glanced over the crowd; she was smiling and waving.

Then, amongst the fans, she saw Archie. The smile left her face. He stood there on crutches, still handsome, with a dark-haired woman on his arm, a pale, slender woman. Archie's eyes caught Gilde's. His face broke into a grin. "Sign my program, please, Mrs. Thornbury," someone said. "Mrs. Thornbury, will you please autograph this for my son?" another said.

She was surrounded by fans. They were all calling out to her at once. For a moment, she felt as if the wind had been knocked out of her, as all the memories of her and Archie, what she had done—the shame she'd brought upon herself—came rushing at her in a surge like a tidal wave.

Gilde felt herself flush. She raised both hands in the air. "I'm sorry to disappoint all of you, but I am not feeling well this evening, so there will be no autographs. However, I want to thank you for coming to see the show. Please know that your support means a lot to me," she said, trying to force a smile. Then she turned around and quickly went back inside the theater.

Her heart beat wildly, and she could barely breathe as she disappeared behind her dressing room door. She dropped into the chair and put her face in her hands. But only a moment later, there was a knock at her dressing room door.

Oh no, she thought. Could Archie have paid someone to let him come backstage?

"Who is it?" she said in a curt voice.

"Miss Thornbury? I have a letter for you." The voice sounded like it was coming from an adolescent boy. *Could the letter be from Archie? How had this young boy gotten backstage? It had to be Archie. He must have paid someone to allow this child to deliver a message to her. That didn't surprise her. Archie—that coward—of course, would send someone else. It was easier to hide behind a letter than to face her. Bastard.*

Gilde had met him when she was in nurses training at the hospital in Birmingham after her first husband, William, had been killed in combat. At the time, she was so lonely and missed William more than she had ever dreamed she could miss anyone.

When she became pregnant and he was released from the hospital, he went back home to his family and abandoned her. That was when Alden, who at the time was her best friend and now her husband, came to her aid. So that she wouldn't face the stigma of being an unwed mother, Alden had proposed to her. But for him, it was more than just a favor to a friend.

At the time, she was still in love with Archie and told Alden as much. She was honest with him, telling him she could promise him nothing. Alden said he didn't expect her to return his love. He was willing to accept her on any terms. When Vicky was born, he cared for her like she was his own. And sometime during those sweet moments, Gilde realized she'd fallen in love with her husband.

When she told him, he was so happy that his joy filled the emptiness Gilde had endured since she left her family behind in Germany. Then, an unexpected turn of events had occurred that changed everything.

One night, she and Alden had gone out for dinner. They were sitting in a restaurant when Gilde ran into Elias, an old childhood friend.

Elias was an orphan, and he'd come to Britain on the Kindertransport, along with Gilde after her parents had been arrested.

Gilde was sent away from everyone she knew and loved and went to live with a family of strangers far away from her home. On the train, she'd ridden beside Elias. The entire trip, she'd leaned on him for support.

That was the first time she'd seen him since they had been separated at the train station when they arrived in Britain. The last time she'd seen him, Elias had been just a boy. Now, he was a handsome man and engaged to an actress. They talked for a while, and he invited Gilde and Alden to a cast party that was being given for the play his fiancée was performing in.

It was at that party that Gilde met her first professional stage director. She'd always loved the theater; she sang and danced as a child. The director was quite taken with her and offered her a small part. From that day on, her life was spinning like a tornado, fast and furious. In fact, she rose quickly and became a star on the London stage.

Gilde steeled herself and got up to open the dressing room door. She took the folded paper. Then she grabbed a few coins from her purse and tipped the star-struck adolescent boy.

She tore open the letter and read:

"I have to see you. There are so many things that you don't know. Things I have to tell you. Things that influenced me to break up with you when I did. But I shouldn't have left you. I made a mistake, Gilde. I love you. Meet me tomorrow at eleven a.m. in front of Big

Ben. I'll be waiting and praying for your forgiveness.
Please show up, Gilde. All I ask is that you give me a
chance to explain."

———

The whole thing made no sense, but at the same time, it made all the
sense in the world. Could she walk away? She'd waited so long,
dreaming that the day would come when she could hurt him the way
he hurt her, but if she did it, she just might get caught in her own web.
And besides that, what the hell was he talking about? What had caused
him to leave her? What were the secrets that she didn't know?

Gilde's life had changed in so many ways since she'd begun to find
popularity in the theater in London. Her voluptuous figure, quick wit,
sharp sense of humor, and strong voice appealed to the audience, and
within a few weeks, it seemed that she had her pick of parts.

Her life was almost perfect. Almost. If she could change one thing,
she would find a way to spend more time with Alden and her daughter, Vicky. In the whirlwind and excitement of living a public life, her
marriage was suffering.

Alden had moved from the hospital in Birmingham to take a job as
a surgeon in London so they could remain together as Gilde pursued
her career. And although he'd done it willingly, she knew he missed
his old job and friends.

Sometimes, when she was alone in her dressing room after a
performance, she wondered if Alden resented her career. How could
he not? Before she'd begun acting, they'd had a beautiful marriage.
Yes, he'd been working long hours, but she had always been there to
greet him when he got home.

Now, she, too, was working long hours, and Vicky was being
raised by a nanny. The life of a performer was exciting, no doubt, but
Gilde wondered if she wasn't giving up precious time with her
daughter and husband—time she would never be able to get back. The

theater, the people, and the fame were all so seductive, but a voice in her mind said, "Be careful, Gilde."

Gilde sat in front of the mirror in her dressing room, staring at the letter in her hand. She had to be out of her mind to go and meet Archie. Why was she even considering it? If she had half a brain, she'd tear this letter to pieces and never show up at Big Ben.

Leave him standing there waiting. That's what he deserved. But she couldn't; she had to know what happened. Curiosity? Was it? Or did she want to hear him beg for forgiveness? He'd hurt her so much, left her so alone and abandoned, pregnant with his child. She needed to hear what he had to say. She wanted to know why and how he could have done this to her. And she wanted to have the chance, finally, to hear him say he loved her and then to tell him to go to hell.

thirteen
Gilde

GILDE SAT with her legs crossed at the knee and her black handbag at her side. She was in the backseat of a taxi wearing dark sunglasses. They were parked across the street from Big Ben. Her long golden hair was caught up in a twist and hidden under a dark hat that hung over her eye, obscuring her face from view. She didn't want Archie to see her first. Gilde wanted to spend a few minutes watching him before she decided whether she would get out of the taxi and talk to him or go back to the safety of her home. However, if she left now, she would never know the answers to the questions that had plagued her since he'd walked out on her.

From the shelter of the cab's backseat, she could see him pacing slowly, unevenly. He walked with a severe limp and a cane from his war injuries. It was probably still painful for him to walk back and forth like that. As she watched, memories of the feelings she had once had for him began tearing at her heart.

After all, even though Alden was the best father any woman could ever hope for, Gilde's daughter's biological father was Archie. As much as she hated him, his sperm had fertilized her egg and created Vicky. Her precious daughter. So, even though Gilde thought Archie was a bastard for having abandoned her when she was pregnant, she still felt a tie to him.

When Archie walked out of her life, he knew she was pregnant. But she had not talked to him since, so she had never told him he had a daughter. Did he have a right to know? The way he'd behaved, he didn't deserve anything. Would he care anyway? He didn't care then. He didn't wonder what would happen when he turned his back on Gilde. He never called to see if his child had survived or been aborted or miscarried. He'd simply disappeared. What a bastard. Gilde sucked in a deep breath and smiled. It felt damn good that she was quickly rising to stardom, and she was glad that he was standing outside while the audience was calling for her. He'd seen her show. Good, she hoped he finally knew what he'd lost.

The hopeless, helpless little Jewish girl, without any family or real friends except for Alden, was on her way to becoming rich and famous. Archie could eat his heart out. When she'd fallen in love with Archie, Alden explained to her that Archie was a Notman, and they were a family of old wealth that would never have accepted a Jewish daughter-in-law from a poor family. But what about a rising star?

Gilde smiled, thinking she was now a force to be reckoned with. She was finally his equal. With that knowledge planted in her brain, Gilde felt her confidence grow. It was time to face Archie. It was time to settle past grievances.

"Thank you," Gilde said, handing the cabbie ten shillings. Then she removed the hat and unpinned her hair, shaking it to her shoulders. With her head held high, she got out of the car and walked towards Archie.

fourteen

Gilde

ARCHIE'S FACE was still undeniably handsome. Even with his cane, he was a glorious specimen of a man.

It had been her husband Alden who had saved Archie's life when he had to remove part of his leg because of the war injury. Gilde had been his nurse after the surgery.

As she walked towards him, Gilde remembered how angry Archie had been at the time. But he'd also been so damn vulnerable, and that had won her heart. Their love affair was one of blind passion. But he'd lied and made promises he never kept. How she'd hated him for what he did. Gilde approached him, and he turned to look at her. Even now, as their eyes met, she felt the color rise on her neck and face. He still had that power over her.

"Gilde." He smiled. "I'm glad you came."

She cocked her head to one side and bit her lip in contemplation. "I came out of curiosity, not love, Archie."

"I don't care why you came. I only care that you are here, and I will finally have a chance to explain."

"I can't wait." Her voice was filled with sarcasm.

"Let's go and have a cup of tea. We can talk," he said.

She nodded. "Yes, let's."

They walked across the street to the closest Lyons tearoom. Gilde suddenly felt a small pang of guilt about meeting Archie. It felt like a betrayal to Alden, their marriage, and their lives. She should have told Alden the truth. They never kept secrets. She should have been honest with him and said she planned to meet with Archie. Alden was the kind of man who would have appreciated the honesty.

Lately, however, she'd been absent from home so much that she felt that she couldn't tell Alden that she was meeting with Archie. He would have taken it as a betrayal. And, although at the beginning of her stage career, Alden had been supportive, he seemed to be slowly growing resentful. The other day, she'd come home late from a show to find him still awake. Alden was sitting on the sofa alone when she entered. He looked up at her, and she saw something in his eyes that troubled her.

"Are you alright?"

"I'm fine," he said.

There were several moments of silence. Then he added, "Gilde, sometimes I feel like I don't know you anymore. You hardly have time for Vicky, and you never have time for us."

"Alden." She took his hand in hers. "I'm sorry. I have just been busy with the show. I know the theater is closed on Monday. Why don't we take Vicky and do something special? Let's think of something very special…"

"I can't. I have to work."

"But you wanted me to make time for us…"

"Everything is always according to your schedule. You pencil me in at your convenience. Our marriage seems to have lost its importance to you."

"Please don't say that, Alden. You know better."

"Do I? I don't know better. I only know what I see."

She was tired that night. Performing drained her. It was too difficult to stand there and argue when all she really wanted was to go to bed.

"I'm exhausted. I can't fight with you now. I'm sorry. Our marriage is a priority to me. It always has been. Try to understand that I have a job that takes up a lot of my energy. Please, try to see my point of view here."

He glared at her. His face told her that he was angry. But she also knew he was hurt.

"I'm sorry..." she said again. "Please, let's talk about this in the morning."

He nodded in agreement without uttering another word. She felt uneasy leaving the room. But at the same time, she was far too spent to continue. So she went to bed.

The following morning, when Gilde got up, Alden had already left for work. They never openly discussed the situation again. However, he made a few comments that she found hurtful, letting her know he was unhappy. Well, how could she blame him?

He had fallen in love with her and married her while she was pregnant with Archie's child. Then, he'd loved little Vicky like his own when she was born.

Alden was so romantic. He was like a knight from a children's book. So gallant, so kind. She loved him. They had been blissfully happy for a while, but then she'd found the theater.

Since she was a child, Gilde had wished to be an actress. But it had always been little more than a dream. Then, once that dream came true, she heard and felt the audience rock the auditorium with applause, and she took that first bow, she was hooked. It was an addiction as strong as alcohol or drugs. When she was performing, Gilde felt a rush of adrenaline that felt like nothing else. A high, a euphoric feeling that was orgasmic.

The waitress came to the table to take their order. She set down glasses of water. Her presence brought Gilde out of her thoughts and back to the present moment.

Gilde and Archie sat at a table by the window. He smiled as he ordered them both tea and pastries.

"So, you wanted to see me? I'm here, Archie. Go ahead, tell me what you've wanted to tell me."

He cleared his throat, and the tea arrived. "I will. I will tell you,"

Archie said, placing his napkin on his lap and running his fingers absentmindedly over his spoon.

Then he looked up into Gilde's eyes and said, "I loved you, Gilde. I still do. But it was my family. I was engaged when I went into the service. My parents expected me to marry my wife ever since we were children. I told my parents about you when I got home. My father threatened to disown me. I would have lost everything, all of my family money, all of my inheritance. My station in life. Gilde … I've never had a job or worked at anything. I wouldn't know how or where to begin. I was afraid. So, I did what they wanted me to do. And the truth is I've been miserable since."

"Do you want me to say I'm sorry for you?"

"I don't expect you to be sorry for me. I was wrong. I left you pregnant and alone." Then he cleared his throat and looked down at the table. "Did you?"

"Did I what?"

"Did you have some sort of help to get rid of the pregnancy? I mean, what happened to the baby?"

She shook her head. "Why the hell do you care?"

"Because I have felt terribly guilty every day since I left you."

"And would you still feel guilty, Archie, if I weren't rich and famous?"

"Yes, Gilde. Yes. I'm glad for you. But yes."

"Hmm." She grunted and looked out the window. "You have a daughter. She's your blood, but she's Alden's child. He was there when she was born. He raised her. Her name is Victoria."

Archie gasped. "My wife can't have children. I believe it's God's way of punishing me."

Gilde said nothing. She stared into his eyes as she sipped her tea.

"You married Alden? The doctor, my doctor, the fellow who did my amputation?"

"Yes."

"You love him?"

"I do. And surprisingly, he came from a family of old wealth, just like you. But the difference between you is that Alden is a man, and you are a leech. You are dependent upon your parents and your family name for everything." Gilde studied Archie, and for the first time, she saw him clearly.

"I thought you were so much better than I was. You were a man of means. Old wealth. Sophistication. I fell blindly for everything I thought you stood for. And I wanted to be a part of your world. But looking at you now. I see you clearly. You're nothing. Less than an ant. Without your parents, you are nobody." Gilde took a deep breath. Her heart fluttered. She felt light and free.

All this time, she'd wondered what would happen if she ever saw Archie again. Would she still be mesmerized by him? Would she find that she was still hopelessly in love with him? No, no, no, not at all. Finally, she could walk out of this café, leave him behind, and not care what happened to him. She was finally free of the memories. A part of her wanted to burst into joyous laughter.

"Do you have anything else you want to say?" Gilde asked, looking directly into Archie's eyes.

"Only that I am happy for you and all of your success. And that I love you. Mum passed last year, and Dad is very ill. I'm unhappy in my marriage, Gilde. Give us another chance. I'm begging you."

Gilde leaned back in her chair. "There was a time when I would have done anything to hear you say those words. But now, well, I am sorry for you. However, I have no romantic feelings for you anymore."

A look of shock washed over his face.

Gilde got up and took her handbag. "Goodbye, Archie," she said, and then as she walked out of the café, she whispered, "Goodbye, forever."

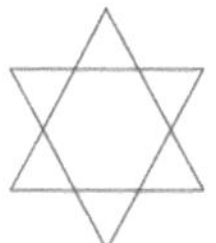

fifteen

Lotti

Berlin
September 1945

BECAUSE YOUTH WAS on her side, Berni's body recovered from the abortion, though not her mind. By the middle of summer, she and Lotti had returned to their jobs at the hotel. Most of the time, Berni was content to leave work and slip quietly back to the safety of the apartment. She walked hunched over and always seemed to be looking at the ground. If anyone tried to talk to her, she was short with them, preferring to be with Lotti or alone.

Lotti was different. No matter what happened, she'd always looked for a bright side. She thrived when she was able to give to others. And now, even with all she'd been through, Lotti still had the need to be of help.

After the fall of the Nazis, Berlin was like a dam that broke with a tidal wave of people flooding into the city every day. Some were survivors who'd been liberated from concentration camps, some had been slave laborers under Nazi rule, while others came back to Berlin after spending years hiding out in the forests, in basements, in attics, or in sewers.

They were Jews and non-Jews; they were political prisoners, prostitutes, Romany, Jehovah's Witnesses, and anyone else who had been considered undesirable. The streets were also filled with newly released prisoners of war, and soldiers with empty eyes on their way home in defeat.

Most of the new arrivals to Berlin were searching for lost loved ones. They were looking for family, friends, neighbors, or anyone from their past.

The clean-up of the debris from the bombings had begun, but it would take time before Berlin could recover. Every day, as Lotti went to and from work, she couldn't help but notice the wanderers on the streets.

How many of them would ever find their friends and families? Would she ever see her brother, Johan, or any of the Margolis family again? Her heart was heavy. It was hard not to be depressed, even though wallowing in self-pity was unusual for Lotti.

One afternoon, she was walking home from work and thinking about the past. Remembering Lev and the time they spent together made her smile but feel sad at the same time. She thought about Michal and Alina and how close they had been. Even little Gilde, although young when she went to Britain, was a part of her extended family. Taavi too. She missed them all terribly but was grateful to have Berni now. At least she had a friend to talk to and share a meal with. It had been much worse before Berni had come to live with her. She'd spent all of her time alone.

A disheveled, dirty woman sitting with a child in her arms on the side of the road was begging for money. Lotti reached into her handbag and took out a few coins.

Look around you, she thought. As she studied the dazed, empty-eyed people who meandered aimlessly through the streets, she thought, *I still have a purpose. There is a reason I am still here. How can I help these people? Instead of feeling sorry for myself, that is what I will do. I will find a way to be of use.*

When Lotti was a young girl before she'd fallen in love with a Jew and disappointed her parents—especially her father—her mother had raised her to be a good Christian. She went to church with her mother every Sunday and was told that when she was sad, the best way to ease her suffering was to help others. That was one of the reasons she'd volunteered at the Jewish orphanage so many years ago, right after her miscarriage. It had helped her to come to terms with the knowledge that she'd never have children of her own, but she could be a surrogate mother to many children who needed one. Her memories of the days at the orphanage were warm and still held a sweet place in her heart. So, that very day, instead of going directly home, Lotti took a train out to the suburbs of Berlin and got a job volunteering two afternoons a week at a displaced persons camp. Perhaps by serving those in need, she would find peace.

Lotti walked into the apartment and put her handbag on the counter. Then she went into the drawer and took out the ration cards. After she put the cards into her purse, she looked for Berni. Berni was sitting in the living room with her legs crossed.

"We have to eat. So, come, let's go and get our rations," Lotti said to Berni.

"I'd rather starve than go out there," Berni said.

"No, you wouldn't. Now come on." Lotti took Berni's hand and pulled her up off the sofa.

"Very well, let's go," Berni said.

Rations were provided by the American soldiers. The soldiers knew that the German women were dependent on them. Most of the soldiers were distant, and some were downright unfriendly. Others were degrading, though some could be openly flirtatious. But Lotti and Berni thought that the hardest on the women of Berlin was a group of American Jewish GIs.

These men made it clear that they controlled the American sector. They were not too fond of the German women. They'd seen fellow soldiers fall at the hands of the Nazis. They'd seen terrible acts of cruelty when they liberated the camps. Berni was afraid of them. Unlike Lotti, she'd never had a close relationship with a Jewish man, and these soldiers were intimidating. She would not go alone to get her rations, so she and Lotti always went together. In many ways,

Lotti feared the American Jews as well. They didn't know her or her background, and when they passed out the rations, it was clear that they did not feel any heartfelt generosity.

Berni cowered like a frightened kitten as she was handed her rations. Sometimes, they made obnoxious comments, and Lotti wanted to put them in their place, tell them what she had endured, and let them know they were not the only ones who had suffered. But they had the power and control of the food, and she dared not make them angry. So, she kept her mouth shut and held Berni's hand until they received their share.

"You know that group of Americans are Jews," Berni said one day. "The soldiers who gave us our rations today."

"Yes, I know," Lotti said.

"I heard a couple of women talking about them. They hate the Jewish Americans the worst of all. That group is a whole unit of Jewish soldiers. And believe me, they resent us even more than the Russians, I think. It's probably because of the concentration camps. Dirty Jewish swine," Berni said.

Lotti stopped dead in her tracks and turned around to look at Berni. She put her hands on Berni's shoulders and stared into Berni's eyes. "Don't ever say that again. Do you hear me? I don't ever want to hear you make another anti-Semitic remark. I can take it from the rest, but not from you." Lotti glared at Berni.

Berni's shoulders went limp. "I'm sorry, Lotti. I really am."

Lotti shook her head. She was at a loss for words. Today, she'd seen a side of Berni she'd never seen before, which scared her. Berni was her only friend, her best friend. But if Berni didn't have a deep-seated hatred for Jews, she would never have thought to make such a terrible remark. Hearing Berni talk that way changed Lotti's view of her friend.

They walked towards home in silence.

The more time Lotti spent at the displaced persons camp, the more despair she felt about finding anyone from her past. The tremendous number of people who had simply disappeared was beyond her comprehension. People were scattered and lost; they didn't know if their loved ones had been murdered in death camps, shot and buried in shallow graves, or, with God's help, were still alive somewhere. And then there was always the question of whether all the people who had gone to hide in the forests knew that the war was over. It was hard to say. At this point, anything could happen. Anyone could be found or not.

Berni and Lotti went together the following week to pick up their rations. Again, a group of Jewish soldiers was standing around in a crowd. Two of them were working with another unit of American GIs, handing out rations.

One man in particular caught Lotti's eye. He reminded her of Lev, but younger, stronger, and far more healthy than Lev had been when she'd last seen him.

This man was muscular, and handsome, with a strong jaw, jutting cheekbones, and a prominent hook nose. His hair was dark, and closely cropped, and his eyes almost black. The soldier was closer in age to Berni than Lotti. And from overhearing him talk to his fellow soldiers while Lotti was waiting in line, she heard one of the other soldiers call him Gabe.

"Next," he said. And to each of the women, he made a cutting comment to remind them that they were at his mercy, taking his charity.

One of the women said, "You're Jewish?"

"Yeah, I am. And I am an American, too."

The woman spit on the ground.

"I'm not going to give you your rations this week," Gabe said.

The woman wrapped her arms around her chest. "I wouldn't want them from you anyway. I'd rather starve."

"I hope you do," the man called Gabe said.

Just then, another soldier came over. "Just give 'em to her, Gabe," he said.

"The bitch can go to hell with the rest of the Nazis," Gabe said.

The other soldier handed the woman her ration cards.

"I hope you choke on it," Gabe said.

When Lotti and Berni reached the front of the line, Gabe handed

Lotti her rations. "It makes me sick that we have to give you food. You don't deserve it. You're all good for nothing Nazis. You pretend that you had nothing to do with what happened to the Jews. But none of you stood up for our people. I saw the camps. I liberated the camps. I was right there and saw what you let them do." Gabe said to Lotti.

Berni looked away, but Lotti's face turned blood red, and she trembled with anger.

"I didn't let them do anything," Lotti said. Her back stiffened. "You don't know anything about me."

Berni pulled on Lotti's sleeve. "Don't start a fight with them. They can cut our rations if they want to," Berni said.

But Lotti shrugged Berni off. She didn't care if she never ate again. Furious, she stared into the soldier's eyes and wouldn't back down.

"You're right. I don't know what you did during the war. But you're not one of us, so to me, it means that you're one of them. I don't know anything about you and your pretty little friend here. But what I do know is that you people are sick bastards."

"That's not fair," Lotti said. She was so heated she wanted to cry. She wanted to throw the ration cards at him and tell him she didn't need his charity. But she couldn't because she did need it, and Berni needed it too. "What you don't know, my American friend, is this…" Lotti took a deep breath, stared into Gabe's eyes, and then spoke in a low growl.

"I was married to a Jewish man. He was my husband, the love of my life, and my best friend. He was killed by the Nazis. They let me live. I would rather have died. Just because I was born a German, don't you dare try to assume I was ever a follower of Hitler." She stared until he looked away. Then she grabbed the bread and ration cards from his hands and walked home.

sixteen
Lotti

THE NEXT TIME Lotti went to pick up her rations, Gabe was there again. There was no other person working the line that day. She grimaced, knowing she would have to be face-to-face with him when she got to the front of the line. It was fall, and the weather was brisk with a slight breeze, but not yet cold. However, she felt chilled and uncomfortable. It was hard to beg for food, especially from a man who hated her.

Lotti didn't feel like fighting again. So when Gabe handed her the rations, she took them and turned away.

"Hey, listen," Gabe said in a soft voice. Lotti stopped and turned around to look at him. "I'm sorry. I thought about what you said last week. And you're right. I don't know what you went through. I was thinking of myself, my people, my friends..." He hesitated, then said, "My family."

"You had family in Germany?" Lotti asked, suddenly feeling bad for him.

"Yeah, my grandparents. I've tried to find out what happened to them. But I can't find any information at all."

"I'm sorry," she said sincerely.

"I liberated a couple of the camps, and when I saw what was there and thought about them being in one of those camps, I don't believe they could have survived."

Lotti felt terrible for this young Jewish man. "I wish there was something I could say. I can't even say I know how you feel. But what I do know is that Hitler took my husband from me. And, my husband was my life."

His eyes met hers, and when she looked into his eyes, they were soft, not hard like he pretended to be.

"Listen, I'm sorry about your husband."

"Yes, so am I."

This time, he didn't throw the food at her. Instead, he was gentle when he handed her the bag of rations.

"Thank you," she said, her head down.

"What's your name?"

"Lotti."

"You're welcome, Lotti."

Two days later, Gabe appeared at the DP camp where Lotti volunteered. He walked over to her and said hello.

"Do you work here?" she asked.

"No, I came to see you."

"Me? Why? How did you know I was here?"

"One of my buddies told me." He smiled. "I wanted to ask you out for lunch, maybe?"

"Oh, I don't know..."

"Come on, what have you got to lose, huh? Listen, I know a wonderful little restaurant. Do you like Jewish food?"

Lotti giggled. "I haven't had Jewish food since Lev passed. Yes, actually I do."

"Well then, let's have lunch. We'll have a little kugel, maybe a knish? What do you say?"

"Oh, I don't know," she repeated.

"For my sake, have lunch with me. Let this be my way of apologizing for being rude," Gabe said.

"Why not?" She smiled. It had been a long time since Lotti had enjoyed a good meal. And it had been even longer since she'd eaten the Jewish cuisine that reminded her so much of the good times she'd shared with Lev. Lotti looked at Gabe in his American army uniform. He certainly was handsome, strong, and self-assured. But he was so much younger than she was.

Besides, Lotti couldn't imagine ever having another man in her life. When Lev died, she felt a part of her heart close forever. But perhaps he would make a nice boyfriend for Berni. After all, she couldn't blame Gabe for being angry and bitter towards the German people. He'd seen the fiendish work of the Nazis firsthand.

But he didn't realize that there were people like Lotti who had never been a part of Hitler's movement. They were, in many ways, just as trapped as the people the Nazis had murdered. The Aryans did have an advantage. If they kept their mouths shut, they would survive. And it was hard to risk death for one's family and one's self for the sake of strangers. Lotti understood this but wasn't sure she could make Gabe understand. She forgave the Germans who were too afraid to speak out, but she could see how Gabe might not.

Because of Lotti's love for Lev, she'd been different from the others. And even though Lotti had not always kept quiet, somehow, she'd been spared by some miracle.

Yes, maybe she would have lunch with him. There were so many things she wanted to say to him, so many things she wanted to explain. Although she had no reason to feel the need to justify her behavior or the behavior of others, for some reason, she still wanted to make Gabe understand. Besides, she would talk to him about Berni while they were eating. Berni needed a companion.

Then Lotti thought about the comment Berni had made about the Jews. Since Lotti wanted to believe the best about people, she tried to convince herself that Berni wasn't really anti-Semitic. It was just that Berni was young and had been through so much. That was what made her say those terrible things about Jews that day. Maybe Lotti could help her. Perhaps, if Berni found someone to love... Lotti smiled to herself as she thought about something Lev once said. "You know," he told her, "helping to bring people who love each other together is a blessing. In Yiddish, we call it a mitzvah."

Lev. She thought of him, and her eyes glassed over. Dear sweet Lev. How she missed him.

seventeen

Lotti

AS GABE PROMISED, the restaurant did serve traditional Jewish cuisine. It had been recently established by two men who were concentration camp survivors. They had developed a bond beyond friendship in Auschwitz and were now working to build a life together.

Before the Nazis invaded Poland, one of the men had been a journalist. When the Jews were sent to the ghettos, he'd been clever enough to bury money before he left. Once he was released, he went back to the site and dug up the money, which was miraculously still there. Then he and his friend took that money and went to Berlin to open a restaurant in the American sector. They had a hunch that the American Jewish GIs would love the place. And they did. The GIs helped the two survivors acquire the supplies they needed. It wasn't fancy, just a small storefront with three scratched-up wooden tables and chairs, a wood floor, and a counter. But the food was good, and it gave the Jewish American soldiers a taste of home.

Lotti and Gabe sat down at the only open table. It was noisy because a line of GIs placed orders at the counter. Gabe got in line. When it was Gabe's turn, Lotti could hear him. Lotti spoke Yiddish; she'd learned it from Lev. Although it was very close to German, Lotti easily recognized the difference. As Gabe told the man behind the counter what they wanted to eat, Lotti realized that Gabe spoke fluent Yiddish.

Gabe waited while the man behind the counter prepared the plates. Then he brought a tray of steaming hot food to the table and sat down.

"So, you were married to a Jewish man?" Gabe said, breaking into her thoughts.

"Yes. I was, and I miss him every day."

Gabe looked directly at her. "They must have made it hard for you. Your neighbors and non-Jewish friends, I mean."

"Some did. Not all. I always figured that if they were my real friends, they would not be anti-Semitic. I couldn't have a friend who hated Jews." Just saying that aloud made Lotti think of the terrible comment that Berni had made. She couldn't forget it. Then she said, "Lev—my husband—and I had Jewish friends, too."

"That's what all the Germans say."

"Gabe, I did. I had close friends who were Jewish. I have no idea what happened to them. Every person who comes to the camp to register, I ask them if they have heard of anyone by the last name Margolis. Taavi, Michal, Alina, even Gilde, although I think Gilde, if she is alive, is probably somewhere in Britain. No one has heard the names. No one ever has an answer."

"These were your friends?"

"Yes, close friends. Very close. My husband was Taavi's best friend and business partner. Michal was his wife. They had two wonderful daughters, Alina and Gilde. Alina and I worked together at a Jewish orphanage. First, Taavi was arrested, and then Michal. When an opportunity came to send Gilde to Britain on the Kindertransport to live with a family, Alina and I decided it was best to send her. These people were a big part of my life. You don't understand, Gabe. Even though they weren't blood, they were my family."

"You haven't heard from any of them?"

"Taavi came to see me once, but it was during the war. I haven't seen him since. Many years ago, Alina and my brother, Johan, moved to Munich. Then, one day, they just disappeared. It was like that, you see. People were gone without any warning, without any reason. Just like that." She looked away as she remembered the last time she spoke to Johan or Alina.

"It's been a long time since I had potato pancakes. You like them?" Lotti said.

"Latkes, yes, of course. We always had them for Hannukah when I was growing up," Gabe said.

"Delicious," Lotti closed her eyes, taking a bite and savoring the taste.

"Yes, the food here is good. Reminds me of my ma's cooking." Gabe smiled. "Hey, I don't mean to be bold, but has anyone ever told you you're beautiful."

Lotti stopped chewing in the middle of a bite and looked directly at Gabe. "You can't be serious." She almost choked.

"Oh, but I am."

"I believe you might be flirting with me." She looked into his eyes, finding it hard to believe what she was hearing.

"Yes, you're right. I'm flirting."

She laughed, "I'm sorry. But that is so funny to me. I'm much too old for you."

"You could let me be the judge of that."

"I could. But I won't. How old are you, Gabe?"

"Old enough to fight in a war. Old enough to liberate two concentration camps," he said as a deep line formed between his brows. "I've seen hell, Lotti. I've seen more than men twice my age and survived."

"I'm thirty-seven, Gabe. And I am still in love with my husband. I've given up on romance. I, too, have experienced many things that made me hard and cold."

"Guarded, maybe. But I don't believe you are hard or cold." He looked at her with eyes the same color as Lev's.

Lotti put her fork down. He'd found her soft underbelly. His tenderness and the color of his eyes brought back a memory of the first time she looked into Lev's eyes. It made her want to weep. She cleared her throat. "I have a roommate. A good friend. She is much younger than I am. I could introduce you," Lotti said, trying to sound cheerful, even flippant.

"I'm not interested in meeting your roommate, Lotti. I am interested in you."

Lotti tried to laugh and make light of what he said, but it touched her too deeply, and her quick giggle came out as a sign of her nervousness. "What would anyone want with me, a woman closer to forty than to twenty and no longer light in her step? No, Gabe, my time for love has passed. The man who owns my heart is dead. So, my heart is dead, too."

"You just give me a chance, will ya? I'll show you that you're wrong. You're still beautiful. You still have plenty of life ahead of you. I'm through here in Germany in less than a year, and I'm going home to Philly. If things work out between us, I sure would like to take you away from Berlin. What would you think about living in America?"

She shrugged. "Just a week ago, you hated me. Accused me of being a Nazi. Now you're thinking about taking me with you to America. Gabe, you are quite an impulsive man."

"Yeah, that might be right. But I see you in a different light now that I know about your life."

"Ah, yes, well, right now, why don't we just enjoy these delicious latkes while they're still hot and crisp."

"Latkes," he said, pronouncing the word with a perfect Yiddish accent. "You say it like a goy. Try again." He laughed. She could see he was teasing her, but not maliciously. He was laughing with her, making it easier for her to laugh at herself. And it had been such a very long time since Lotti had allowed herself to laugh.

"Latkes," she said again. "Was that better?"

"Yeah, a little," he said. "Looks like we're gonna have to spend a lot more time together if you're ever going to perfect that Yiddish accent."

She shook her head, but she couldn't resist smiling.

eighteen
Gilde

London
October 1945

BY THE TIME Gilde got out of bed, it was almost noon. Alden had gotten up early to take care of Vicky. They'd hired a nurse to care for the child because Gilde was almost never home, but Gilde had forgotten that she'd given the nurse the day off.

Gilde had attended a cast party the night before and had too much to drink. Last night was just another one of those wild affairs where her theater crowd of very talented people got together at one of their homes and competed for the starring role. Even offstage, they were always performing. They sang ballads, recited Shakespearean monologues, tap-danced, dressed outrageously, and collectively drank enough alcohol to keep a liquor store in business for at least a month.

Alden never went to the parties. He always begged off. He was either at work or claimed he had to stay home with Vicky. Gilde knew he hated all the noise, so she never pushed him to join her. Today, she would have to endure the aftereffects. Her head ached, and her stomach was queasy, but she picked Vicky up and held her in her arms.

"You're off today?" Gilde asked Alden.

"No, I'm working tonight at the hospital." He had been reading the newspaper. He did not look up at her when she spoke to him. Instead, he kept the paper covering his face.

"I wanted to talk to you about something," Gilde said.

"That's interesting because I've wanted to talk to you too."

"You first, Alden."

"No, go ahead, Gilde," he said, putting the paper down on the table. She saw a flash of sadness in his eyes. Then, as was Alden's way, he gave her his full attention.

"I'm going to contact Elias. I'm hoping he can help me get into Berlin to see Lotti. I've told you about Lotti and Lev. Theirs is the only address I have of anyone from my past."

"Oh, good," he said. Then Alden got up and walked over to sit beside Gilde. He took her hand in his, but he was looking at the floor. Alden cleared his throat. "I want a divorce," he said

She couldn't believe what she was hearing. Her eyes flew open wide. "What, Alden. Why?"

"Because I thought I could make you love me. But I was wrong. For a while, things were really good, but then you got involved with the theater, and now I never see you."

"I love you. But, the theater… well, it's my work."

"I know, but it's also your true love. And it's hard to have two loves, Gilde."

She stood up and put the baby down on her blanket. Then she walked to the window. She was afraid to ask this question, terrified of his answer. But she had to know. "Is there someone else?"

"I've met someone. Yes."

"Oh my God, Alden. Who is she?"

"A nurse. She works with me. At first, we were just friends. But then, Gilde, you have been so distant, distracted."

"A nurse? At the hospital with you? Do I know her? What's her name?"

"I don't think you know her, Gilde. Her name is Jane. Jane Kendall."

"Oh my God," Gilde said, sinking into the sofa. Vicky started to cry, but Gilde couldn't pick her up. She didn't trust her arms to be steady enough to hold her child. "Jane Kendall? Jane Kendall?"

"Yes."

"I know her, Alden. I lived with her and her family when I came over on the Kindertransport from Germany to London. Her family died in a bombing. I haven't seen her since. Now this? Does she know you're my husband?"

"Yes. She knows. She was so sorry to hurt you. God, I am sorry to hurt you. It's just that I was alone so much, and she was always there. You belong on the stage, Gilde. Life with me is too small for you."

Gilde felt her stomach turn over. Jane. Oh God, Jane had once been her dearest friend. When she first got to London, Jane was her lifeline. In fact, she'd shared everything with Jane, things she'd shared with no one else.

Jane, her best friend, her sister of the heart. The betrayal was like a butcher's knife plunged through her very soul. Jane.

nineteen
Gilde

GILDE SAT in the living room while Alden went into the bedroom and packed a bag. She could hear him taking the suitcase from the closet shelf.

All of her ambition and drive to become a star had evaporated. She'd never felt so lost or alone. If she had the courage, she would go into that room and beg him to stay. Alden had been the only stability she had in her life. But he no longer loved her. And even worse, he was in love with Jane.

Vicky was crying in her room. She'd awakened from a nap, and Gilde knew that if she didn't go in and pick her up, Vicky would continue to wail until she either vomited or fell asleep. However, Gilde's heart was so heavy that it was impossible to move from the sofa.

A million thoughts were going through her mind. What would she have done without Alden, without his quiet support for everything she had done? Yes, she loved her work, and yes, the applause of an audience was exhilarating. But nothing ever meant as much to her as her husband. Alden was different from all the other men in her life. Alden was not only her lover; he was her best friend.

Vicky was howling now. Gilde pushed herself off the couch and went to get the baby. Vicky must have felt Gilde's sadness because when her mother took her into her arms, Vicky cried even harder.

"Shhhh, Gilde whispered and tried to sing a lullaby to the child, but her voice was strained.

Before he left, Alden came into the room. Gilde bit her lower lip. Her body was trembling. The door was ajar, and from where she sat, Gilde could see Alden's suitcase packed and ready to go. *My God. Don't leave me.*

"I'm leaving now, Gilde. I'm sorry, and you know I only wish you the best in everything. You're on your way to becoming a star. This is what you were meant to do."

She looked at him, his hair tousled the way it always was, and she wanted to run into his arms and beg him to stay. But she was afraid he would reject her, and she couldn't bear the pain, so she just stood there looking at him.

His lips formed a kiss. Then he smiled sadly and left the apartment, closing the door softly behind him. Gilde felt as if a part of her had died at that very moment.

twenty
Gilde

October 1945

AFTER ALDEN LEFT HER, Gilde lost interest in everything. She quit the theater, gave her current role to her understudy, and sank into the depths of depression. She had been performing a supporting role in a romantic musical. Her character had just fallen in love and was singing her heart out about how overcome she was with joy. It would have been impossible for Gilde to go on playing this role in the state of mind she was in since Alden left.

Alden and Jane. Thoughts of them as a couple rolled around in her mind constantly, and she was miserable. Nothing, not even little Vicky's smile, could soothe her. How had she let this obsession with the stage steal the true happiness from her life?

What had once seemed so important now meant nothing. Days passed, and she didn't bathe or wash her hair. Even though she was at home all the time, she still had a nurse to take care of Vicky. She wondered if Alden thought of her or of Vicky. She wondered if he ever missed the good times they shared. Somehow, she'd lost her way, and she wished she'd never met Elias's girlfriend, who had opened the door to this magical world of the theater for her.

Gilde tried drinking to obliterate the pain, but it didn't work. She hated the taste of alcohol and couldn't consume enough to help her forget. Her mind was always racing, and she continuously chastised herself for her mistakes.

The war was over. The only thought that could bring her heart the slightest joy was finding her parents and her sister again. That and, of course, little Vicky. Thus far, Gilde had been avoiding a trip back to Germany because she was afraid she might have to face the fact that they had all perished, and the idea was unbearable. But now, she decided she was going to try to find them.

Vicky needed a family. And with Alden gone, so did she—desperately. From what she'd heard, travel to Berlin was nearly impossible. The trains were not going through directly. She decided to call Elias. He had military connections; perhaps he could help her get to Berlin. Although she couldn't be sure what she would find when she got there, she was willing to try.

"Elias, it's Gilde."

"Gilde? How are you?"

"I'm all right, I guess."

"And the husband, the little girl?"

"Vicky's fine. Alden left me."

"Oh? I'm sorry. Yeah, well, things like that happen, I guess. Babs left me, too."

There was silence for several seconds

"I'm sorry to hear it, Elias."

"Yeah, well, me too."

"I don't know how to ask you this, but I need a favor," Gilde asked.

"Sure? What is it?" he said.

"I want to go back to Berlin and find my family."

"Gilde." He didn't speak for a while. She thought the line had gone dead. Then he said, "Listen. It's hard to get into Berlin. Very hard. And, even worse, there's no telling what you're going to find. Besides, where would you go? Where would you begin to look?"

"I'd go back to my house."

"From what I understand, most of the homes of Jewish families were confiscated by the Nazis. They gave them to German families."

"What? Are you sure?"

"Yeah, I sure am. And the businesses, too. I mean the Jewish-owned businesses. So your father's business is probably gone."

"Lotti and Lev. That's where I'll go. I'll go to their house. They'll know where my parents and my sister are."

"Yes, well..."

"Well, what, Elias?"

"I don't know how to tell you this, but most Jews didn't survive. I am sure you have heard about the concentration camps and the death camps. It's all true, Gilde. I'm sorry."

Her empty heart was already bleeding, and this wound only made the pain more severe. "I have to go. I have to try, Elias. They are all Vicky and I have now that Alden is gone."

He didn't answer for several minutes. She'd thought they'd lost the connection. "Elias?"

"Yes, I'm here. Gilde, the trains aren't running from London to Berlin. If you're really serious about this, you'd have to take a train to Harwich and then take a ferry across to Rotterdam. You'd have to try to get to Berlin by land from Rotterdam. It sure as hell won't be easy, and then there is the Soviet Occupation zone to contend with. All I can say is I don't recommend trying to get to Berlin right now. Besides, if by some miracle, you do make it there, Berlin is a disaster area from the bombings. It's total chaos. I just don't think it's a good idea. It's not safe, Gilde, at least not now."

Gilde collapsed into the chair by the phone and sat in silence. Then she cleared her throat. "I understand, Elias. I suppose I'll have to wait."

After she hung up the receiver, Gilde laid her head on the table and let the tears come. She wished she could talk to Alden. If only she hadn't taken her marriage for granted. It had been a short time since she quit the theater, and the fans had already forgotten her. What a fickle business. What a fool she was to have let true happiness slip through her fingers.

After checking on Vicky to see that she was asleep, Gilde lay on her bed. How could she ever silence the voices in her mind?

Someone knocked at her bedroom door.

"Come in," Gilde said.

"Mrs. Thornbury. I don't know if you remember, but you said I could have tomorrow off." It was Vicky's nanny with her cockney accent.

"Yes, that's fine," Gilde said, feeling more like screaming than talking.

"Do you want me to stay, Mrs. Thornbury? I can stay if you need me."

Gilde shook her head. "No. Are you going to leave tonight?"

"Well, I sure would like to. I mean, if it's all right with you."

"Yes, it's fine," Gilde said. She heard the curt sound of her voice and immediately regretted being rude. "I'm sorry, Meredith. I didn't mean to be so short with you. I'm not feeling well."

"Then I won't go, ma'am."

"No, no, please go. I insist that you do." Gilde took one pound out of her purse. "Here, here is a bonus for you," she said as she handed it to Meredith.

"Thank you so much, ma'am," Meredith stammered, overwhelmed by Gilde's generosity.

Gilde smiled, but tears threatened to spill from her eyes. How was she ever going to go on without Alden?

"Make sure you lock the door on your way out," Gilde said.

After Meredith left, Gilde couldn't fall asleep. She sat by the window and listened to the silence, and in the silence, she heard her parents' voices. They didn't speak directly to her. They were only the voices of memory, of things that had happened so long ago. She could hear Alina's laughter, but she could not remember her face or Lotti's or her parents'. Their features had blurred in her memory.

As she sat looking outside, Gilde quietly sang to herself. She sang the simple songs her father had sung to her and her sister when they were very young.

"You've got to have a little Mazel because Mazel means good luck.

You'll always have good luck if you have a little Mazel." She sang it in a whisper, but it brought tears to her eyes, and they flowed freely down her cheeks.

"Where is my Mazel, Papa? I have no good luck. I lost you and Mama and Alina. I lost William and his family. I have no heart to go back to my career. And worst of all, Papa, I lost my rock, my oak tree, my Alden. I don't have any Mazel." She put her head down on her arm and wept softly.

Gilde got up and poured herself a shot of brandy. She hated alcohol; the taste was terrible, but she downed it and then another. The warmth helped to calm the pain and emptiness inside of her.

After three straight shots, she laid her head back down and closed her eyes. Then Gilde fell into a deep sleep. By some miracle, Vicky slept, too. And it wasn't until she heard a loud knocking on the door that she awakened. *Meredith will get the door.* But then she remembered that she'd given Meredith the time off. Her neck ached from sleeping in an uncomfortable position. There was another knock, and she forced herself to get up.

"Who is it?" she said, still groggy with sleep from the alcohol.

"It's me. Your husband. It's William."

William? Gilde felt her knees grow weak and begin to wobble. Her heart fluttered in her chest. She flung the door open.

"William? You're alive?"

He nodded. She fainted.

twenty-one

Alina

New York
November 1945

ALINA SAT at her desk in the office she'd built adjacent to her bedroom and began doing her weekly payroll. She'd designed the placement of the furniture so that she had a good view of Joey's room, making it easy to keep an eye on him while she worked.

On top of the whitewashed desk were two piles of neatly organized papers. Alina kept accurate records to ensure everyone received the correct commissions each week. The girls constantly talked amongst each other about how fair Alina was to them. They discussed how she always paid them in full and on time. Alina often overheard the conversations.

The girls often spoke harshly about the past when they had worked at other houses. The owners, they said, would find ways to keep some of their money, making false claims, saying that they owed extra for this or that. Alina prided herself on treating the girls the way she would have wanted to be treated. She was at the brothel all the time, and although she didn't sleep with the men, it was easy to imagine how hard the job was and what the prostitutes had to endure every day. She knew that they had no other options. There was a time when she had been in a situation where she couldn't see any option but to marry Trevor, and it was terrible to feel trapped. If this were their only way to earn a living, Alina would make sure that at least they were treated properly.

There was a knock on Alina's door.

"Come in," Alina said, putting the pencil behind her ear. A habit she'd developed because she always seemed to misplace her pencil.

"I brought you a cup of coffee." It was Klara.

"Oh, thanks. I could use that." Alina smiled, taking the cup and sipping the hot, fragrant liquid.

"I have news. Maybe you want to know, maybe not," Klara said.

It was early morning, and Klara hadn't done her hair or makeup yet. When she wasn't made up, she looked young and almost innocent. All except for the striking ruby-red hair.

"Don't tease. What's the news."

"Well…" Klara said, then took a moment to sip of coffee.

Alina gave her a mock frown for holding the news back. "Come on, tell me."

"Yesterday, I went into town to buy some fabric for that black velvet dress May will be making for me."

"Yes, and?"

"And, in the Russian community, news travels rather fast. Now, as you already know, the women don't talk to me because of my life of sin, of course." She laughed.

"Of course." Alina shrugged.

"However, I overheard two women talking. I am sure they were talking loud enough so that I could hear them."

"Go on, what?"

"They said Ugo is back in New York. He's home from the war. He made it through. He survived. He's alive."

Alina gasped. She hoped that was what Klara had come to tell her. "Oh, thank God," Alina whispered. "Is he alright? Was he hurt?"

"I don't know, they didn't say. But what I do know is that he is alive. And…"

"And?"

"You love him, Alina. We both know you do."

"He is your ex-husband, Klara."

"Ugo is more like a brother to me than he ever was like a husband. We were young when we were sweethearts. He and I discovered sex. But I'm not the same girl I was in Russia, and I don't want the same things. I care for Ugo, and I always will. I know he resents me. And I can understand his feelings. But he shouldn't. He knew when he got to America that we had grown apart. It was obvious to both of us. He resents that I have become a prostitute. He can be so self-righteous sometimes. But the important thing is, I care for you, my friend. You've done a lot for me, Alina. More than you know. I want you to be happy. And I know you and Ugo love each other."

"Yes, well, I don't think it's in the cards for me to ever be happy in love. Ugo could never accept that I won't give up the house. He doesn't understand why I need security so badly. So, that's that. But, thank God he is alive."

"Yes, thank God."

twenty-two
Alina

ALINA AWAKENED, choking and coughing. She was disoriented from a lack of air. It was dawn, and the sun had just begun to rise. From her bed, she could see the rays poking through the charcoal smoke that was so thick in her room that she could not see the floor. Her head was heavy. She felt dizzy, and for a moment, she was confused. Then her heart began to race, and she realized that the house was on fire. Her first thoughts were for Joey. She heard the roar of fire and the screams from the girls. Why hadn't she heard them before? Was her head that clouded? She jumped out of bed. "Joey!" she screamed. "Joey!"

Alina knew the house well, yet it was as if she was lost. The smoke had filled the house quickly, and now the room was black. She could no longer see any light coming in from outside. Under such a heavy black cloud, it felt impossible for her to navigate to the room adjacent to hers. She was bumping into furniture. She even stubbed her toe on something she couldn't see. A pain shot up her leg, but she ignored it. Alina had to get to her son.

She couldn't remember where she'd heard this, but someone had once said to get down on your belly and crawl through a fire. The smoke would be less thick. It was nearly impossible to see even a few feet before her, so she dropped to the ground and began to creep on her hands and knees. Finally, she found her way to Joey's room. He had not awakened. Alina could not stop coughing. Her eyes and nose were running profusely. Yet Joey wasn't coughing at all. He was silent. Fear shot through her like a lightning bolt. Her entire body was trembling. *Was he dead?* Alina shook her son hard. Hoping she could force the life back into him. "Mama's here," she said, lifting him from the bed and carrying him towards the door. She tripped over the rug on the floor and fell forward, dropping Joey. He awakened coughing and frightened. "Mama, help me."

"I'm here, Joey. I'm here." She could barely talk or catch her breath. But she thanked God that he spoke. *Joey was alive.* She felt a strong wave of gratitude even in the middle of a terrible fire. *I thought I'd lost him.*

"Alina." It was Klara. She'd come to Alina's room to help her. "Alina."

"I'm in here. I'm trying to get Joey outside."

"Let me help you."

Alina carried Joey. Klara held Alina's hand and pulled her along as they began to push forward through the burning building. Wooden boards from the structure of the house fell into the flames before them. Still, they kept trying to get through. As they passed the kitchen, an explosion rocked the structure and sent them both flying.

"Joey!" Alina screamed.

"Over here, Mama." At least he was alive. Her chest ached, but she found her way to him. "Klara?"

"I'm here, Alina."

Alina couldn't see Klara. "Where are you?"

"With Joey."

Alina followed the sound as best she could until she was with her son and Klara. It was only a few feet from the door. Lifting her son and grabbing Klara's arm, Alina headed to the exit. *Watch out for the big overstuffed chair,* Alina reminded herself. Then they were outside.

Alina fell on the grass, still holding Joey. The fresh air filled her lungs, and she coughed even harder. In fact, Alina coughed until she vomited black mucus. Then she looked at Joey. His face was covered with soot, and he wasn't breathing.

twenty-three

Alina

THREE GIRLS DIED THAT NIGHT. They were young women. Alina felt sick about it, but she felt responsible. Joey was taken by ambulance to the hospital, where Klara and Alina stayed with him.

"He's alive, but he's not a strong boy. You already know that, I'm sure," the doctor told Alina.

"Yes, I know. He had polio when he was very young." Alina stiffened her back. Klara put her arm around her friend for support. "Will he live?"

The doctor shrugged. "His lungs are weak, and to be quite truthful with you, I'm surprised he made it through the fire. However, we'll do our best."

"Can I go in and see him?"

"Yes, go on, he's down the hall in room twelve."

Alina's heart felt like it was crushed when she looked at Joey, dwarfed by the large white hospital bed. She could only see the sad shape of his deformed hips and legs that lay beneath the blanket. A nasal catheter fed oxygen into his tiny nostrils, and his small chest rose and fell with the shallow intake of his breathing. Blue veins covered his closed eyelids and lips, and his small fingernails were slightly blue.

Klara took Alina's hand in hers and squeezed it. Alina glanced at Klara, then reached out and touched Joey's small fingers and caressed them.

"Joey, Mama's here," she whispered, putting her face close to his. He didn't respond. "Joey?"

Joey's eyes flickered open, and although Alina couldn't be sure, she thought she saw a smile drift across his face before he closed his eyes and was once again unreachable.

Klara sat beside Joey's bed with Alina for several hours until night fell. Then she turned to Alina. "I am returning to the house to see how badly it's been damaged. I'll be back tomorrow."

Alina nodded. The house. She'd forgotten about the house. "Yes, thank you, Klara."

twenty-four
Klara

WHEN KLARA ARRIVED BACK at the brothel, she immediately saw nothing to salvage. All was lost. She sank onto the concrete stoop and put her head in her hands. Things had been going so well for her, for Alina, in fact, for all the girls. Nobody wanted to be a prostitute; however, for most of the girls, this house and this job were as good as they could ever hope for.

Right now, Klara and Alina were in trouble, and they would need money. Several months prior, Alina had shown Klara the dresser drawer in her bedroom where she kept her money. "I want you to know where the money is in case anything ever happens to me," Alina had told her. "You are the only person I can trust to take care of Joey if I die."

Klara had dismissed Alina's serious comment at the time. "You are young, and you are not going to die."

But looking through the skeletal remains of the building, Klara could see that the money was gone, burned with the house. The dresser was nothing but ashes. Alina was penniless. Klara had spent her money quickly, but now all her belongings were lost. She had a couple of dollars in her pocket, and that was all she had left. Well, no sense in worrying about all of that right now. Right now, she had to come up with an idea to help Alina and herself and somehow rebuild the house. But how? With no money, how could they start over?

Then, sitting on the stoop with the smell of smoke still lingering in the air, Klara got an idea.

The first thing she did was go to the hospital and talk to Alina.

"I have to go away for a few days. I am going to see an old customer of mine to see if he can give us a loan to rebuild the house."

"You saw the house?" Alina asked.

"Yes."

Alina shook her head. "It was that bad?"

"It's gone. Destroyed."

"Did you check my dresser? Was the money there?"

"It was burned. The dresser was burned to ashes, Alina."

Alina felt sick. She was sitting beside Joey, watching the rise and fall of his chest. God, if she lost him, she didn't know what she would do. The house was less important, far less important. But it meant everything to the girls. And besides, where was she going to go now? How was she going to earn a living?

"Was anyone else hurt?"

"Three of our girls died, but you already know about them. Rose, Mary, and Andrea. I told Rosey's family… they had disowned her long ago, but her mama cried anyway. After all, the girl was just sixteen years old." She shook her head. "It could have been any one of us."

Klara patted Alina's hand. "Anyway, I tried, but I couldn't find any family for Mary or Andrea. Maybe their families are still overseas. Oh, Alina, what a terrible way to die. I think of those girls, and I feel sick to my stomach. Poor souls. I don't think I'll ever get the stench of that burning building out of my nose. It's lingering like a nightmare you can't wake up from. Well, at least none of the customers was hurt. The rest of our employees are scattered. I couldn't find May. For now, they're all probably looking for work somewhere else."

Alina frowned. "It will take forever to rebuild the house, and unless your customer can help us financially, we can't do it. We have no money. Every dollar I had was in that house."

"I know."

Alina nodded. "I suppose you have to go and see your client," Alina said, fighting the tears.

"Yes. But I'll be back. Where can I find you?"

"I'll be here in the waiting room. I don't even have enough cash to go to a flop house. Would you believe I've even thought about contacting Ugo and asking him for help? At least just for enough money until I can find some kind of work. With things being the way they are, I might have to work as a prostitute, too."

"Oh, Alina. You've been my best friend. Prostitution is no life for you. You aren't made for it. That would be a last resort. Let me try to talk to my customer and see if he will help us out. I'll be back as soon as I can, I promise. And I'll do my best not to let you down."

twenty-five
Klara

KLARA TOOK the subway to a small neighborhood tavern tucked between two brownstones on the Lower East Side. Roger had taken Klara to this place for drinks a few times. Although Roger had never come out and told her what he did for a living, rumors ran rampant in the house that he was a hitman for the mob. Plenty of lawyers, judges, and policemen in the throes of passion shared information with the girls they might have otherwise kept confidential.

Because of his job, Klara had kept Roger at a distance. She was afraid of him. He maimed and killed for a living. But, unlike so many of her other clients, Roger had wanted more from her than just casual sex in exchange for money. He didn't treat her as if she had been ruined. Roger didn't look at her as if prostitution had made her unsuitable to be a part of his life outside of the safe confines of the brothel.

In fact, several times, he'd tried to convince her to leave the house and become his exclusive girlfriend, his mistress. And he wasn't ashamed to be seen with her in public. He took her out for dinner and drinks. Sometimes, Klara almost felt as if he were trying to court her. The very idea had made her laugh a little. But not today. Today, she was not amused. Today, she needed help, and of all the clients who'd come to have sex with her, she was pretty sure Roger was the only one who would come through with any real help.

"I am looking for Roger. You know the big guy with the dark hair?" she asked the bartender.

"Yeah, who are you?"

"You don't remember me? I was in here with him before."

"I see a lot of people. I make it my business not to remember anything. You understand?" the bartender said.

"Well, you need not worry about telling me where Roger is. I can promise you that Roger would be happy to see me," Klara said. Her English was broken, but she'd learned enough of the language from talking to her customers over the years to communicate fairly well with Americans.

"Roger isn't here."

"Where is he?"

"How the hell should I know. You got his phone number?" The bartender looked at her skeptically.

"Actually, yes, I do."

"Then call him."

"Please… I don't know how to ask you this, but I have no money. My house burned down, and I need to ask Roger for help."

"Well, he can't help you right now because he's not here. So, call him tonight." The bartender picked up a dirty rag and began to wipe the bar down.

"But I have no place to sleep tonight," Klara said, clearing her throat.

"That's not my problem. I got my own problems."

Klara glared at the bartender, and then she left. She took the subway to a very wealthy client's home. Never in all the years that she'd been working as a prostitute had she ever gone to the home of a customer. It was understood that she should keep her distance from her clients' lives outside the brothel. But she'd broken all the rules since the fire had flung her and Alina into a whirlpool of desperation.

This one had a sick wife, and he'd been coming to see Klara for several years before she moved from her previous place of employment to Alina's house. He seemed kind and understanding. She hoped he would be willing to give her a few dollars to help her get through the night. Then, tomorrow, she'd call Roger.

Klara rang the bell.

He came to the door in a robe. His hair, which was usually neatly combed to cover his bald spot, was askew. "What are you doing here?"

"I need help."

"Don't ever come near my house or my family," the client said, his voice a low, threatening growl.

"Daddy, who is it? Who is at the door?" A teenage girl's voice floated in from the back of the house.

"Just someone selling something, sweetheart.

"How dare you show up at my house. I pay you money to be discreet. You're never supposed to show up at my home. Get out of here right now." He went to slam the door, but Klara held it open.

"Give me a few dollars, and I'll disappear. If you can do that, I'll never come back. I'll never bother you again. I need money desperately. The brothel burned down last night. I have nowhere to stay, no place to go."

"Here." He flung ten dollars at her and then slammed the door.

Klara stuffed the cash in her pocket. She was humiliated, but what did she expect? She knew when she started working as a whore that men would treat her this way. It shouldn't hurt her feelings, but it did. Klara squared her shoulders. No reason to dwell on the pain. It wouldn't change things. This was what she'd chosen. Her heels clicked as she walked down the pavement, stairs, and subway and rode back to the hospital.

Alina was still in the hospital room with Joey, but the visiting hours were almost over. Klara knew Alina would be told to leave very soon.

"Take this and get a cheap room for the night." Klara handed Alina a few dollars. "Eat something, too."

"Oh no, I can't take this," Alina said.

"You have no choice," Klara said. "I've struggled my entire life. I know what it means not to have a choice, and right now, Alina, you have no choice. I'll be back in a couple of days."

twenty-six
Klara

KLARA TOOK the money she had in her pocket and went to the pharmacy. There, she bought a bottle of dark brown shoe polish. Then she went to the thrift store and purchased a modest dress that made her look innocent and a pair of heavy sensible shoes that looked like they belonged to a librarian.

From there, she walked to the subway station and entered the bathroom. When she was sure she was alone, she opened the shoe polish. She spread it over her long red hair, carefully covering it completely. The results were a dull, dark brown color. It made her look serious and plain. She removed all traces of makeup from her face. Then she put on the dress and the sensible shoes. Now, she was no longer glamorous or memorable. She looked in the mirror and trembled for a moment. *I'm almost ugly*, she thought. But, of course, her plan was in progress, and this was just the way she'd wanted to appear.

With her dark hair and simple dress, Klara walked through the streets of New York, overlooked and ignored. She stopped at a phone booth and slipped in, closing the door behind her. Taking a small piece of paper out of her purse, she carefully matched the shape of the numbers on the dial to the numbers on the paper. She could not read them, but she could compare how they looked. Then the phone began to ring. Her heart pounded, and she had to hold on to the side of the phone booth while waiting for an answer.

"Hello."

Thank God, it was Roger. She recognized his voice immediately; it was strong, male, and raspy.

"Roger. It's Klara. You know, Klara, from Alina's house?"

"Of course, doll face. I would recognize that accent anywhere. You're the sexy Russian dame with hair the color of a wildfire."

"I hate to ask this of you. But once, when we were together, you said that if I ever needed anything, I could call you," she said timidly.

"Sure, what do you need?"

"Roger, it's something very serious. I mean, it's not legal. But, well, I really need help."

"I'll tell you what. I ain't worried about the legal part. But how about we make a deal? You and I spend some time together, like a week or so, maybe take a trip to the ocean? Have a little fun. What do you say? And in exchange, I'll do the favor. Whatever it is…"

"You are taking this seriously, I hope."

"Yeah, of course. You don't believe me?"

"Two weeks on the ocean? Just the two of us. I'll make sure you are happy, Roger. I promise you won't regret helping me. I'll reward you very well," she said in her breathiest, sexiest voice.

"Sounds good to me. I can put money on the fact that I know you will come through, and it will be a wild ride. Now go ahead and tell your sugar daddy just what it is that you need," Roger said.

And so she did.

twenty-seven

Klara

KLARA KNEW WHERE TREVOR LIVED. Although she had no proof, she believed in her heart that Trevor was responsible for the fire. She was going to pay Trevor a visit, one he would remember. Klara ran down the stairs to the subway. Handing the man at the booth a few coins, she went through the turnstile and got on the train to take her to Trevor's house.

"Good afternoon," Klara said when Trevor opened the door. "My name is Vera. I have been going up and down the street in your neighborhood looking for work as a maid. I am a very efficient housekeeper. I can cook, sew, and wash. And"—she hesitated momentarily, then smiled her most fetching smile at Trevor—"I must admit I was not expecting such a handsome man to answer the door here." She cast her eyes down. "Please, if you need help to keep your house, sir. I am in desperate need of work. I am all alone in this country and have no one to turn to and no money."

She played coy, acting as if she could hardly speak the language. But having been a prostitute, she was cunning with the use of her eyes and body language to charm a man. All men loved to be complimented, she thought.

"You said you are all alone, which means that you have no children. Am I correct? I am assuming you would want to live in?"

"I have no children. And, yes, I need a place to stay. It's dangerous for a girl alone on the streets, and I am a modest girl with morals. You understand me?"

Trevor studied the girl. When Alina had lived with him, he'd gotten used to having someone take care of his cooking, laundry, and cleaning, and he'd been having trouble managing the house since she'd left. That was one of the reasons he'd hired someone to burn down that whorehouse. She'd made him dependent on her and then had the audacity to steal money from him and leave him without a thought.

But of course, that wasn't the only reason he'd gotten rid of that embarrassment of a business she built. She was publicly humiliating him. His wife, the owner of a brothel. What kind of man would that make him? How weak he would appear to people. It would seem that he had no control over Alina, and a man should have control over his wife. And, he figured, the greatest benefit of burning down that house was that if she lost her business, she'd come crawling back to him on her hands and knees. After all, she was still his wife. Even better, if by some miracle the kid died in the fire because he was so weak anyway, well, then things between Alina and him would certainly improve. They might return to how they were before she'd given birth to the child. But for now, he could hire this woman until Alina returned to her rightful place as his wife. Then, when Alina comes begging on his doorstep, he would decide whether to allow her to come home or not. Vera was young and attractive, with no children, thank God, and she seemed to know her place. Well, why not have someone take care of things for him? It would make his life easier, and he could afford it.

"I will pay you two dollars a week. You will work six days. I expect you to keep the house clean and the laundry pressed, and I take my meals at seven a.m., noon, and six o'clock. I meet with a group of fellows on Tuesdays for a card game, so I will be gone for dinner. Therefore you will not be required to prepare my meal. However, every fourth Tuesday, the same gentlemen will come to my home, where I will host the card game. I expect you to prepare a nice spread for them. I will provide the money for you to purchase the proper food, but you must do a good job preparing it. Can you do all of this and do it well?"

"Yes, yes, sir." Klara smiled fetchingly. She couldn't tell if he was attracted to her or not. His face was guarded. But he'd hired her, and tomorrow was Tuesday. Hopefully, the card game was not at his house.

"Would you like me to go shopping for food for tomorrow? Are the gentlemen coming to your home, or will you be going out?"

"I will be going out tomorrow. It will be my turn to host in three weeks. No need to concern yourself with that dinner just yet. However, I will know if your cooking meets my requirements by then. It will give us some time to see how well you do with everything," Trevor said, opening the door.

She smiled at him and walked into the house. So, Klara thought, this was where Alina had lived. And this was where she had suffered so terribly. Well, Trevor was going out tomorrow night. What luck!

twenty-eight
Klara

THE FOLLOWING AFTERNOON, Trevor left at four o'clock for his card game. As soon as he was gone, Klara went into his office and searched his file cabinet. It took her over an hour, but she was sure she had found what she was looking for—a copy of his will. She opened it. She couldn't read the words, but what she was able to read was Alina's name. She'd seen it in print many times, and there it was on paper that she assumed was his will. So, Klara hoped she was right, and Trevor had not yet removed Alina as his beneficiary. Her heart was racing. *Please, let this be the right document*, she thought. Then she took a deep breath. She would need to act fast.

Klara got Roger's number out of her handbag and picked up the phone. Just then, the doorbell rang. Should she answer it? Who could it be? She didn't want anyone to know she was even there. Only she and Trevor knew of her existence then. It rang again. Her heart felt like it would jump out of her chest. She waited for a third ring, but it didn't come. Finally, silence. Klara had never done anything like this before. She thought the black telephone receiver felt cold and hard in her hand, almost like a gun, and then she shivered.

Carefully, she matched the numbers on the paper to the numbers on the phone. As she did, she cursed herself for refusing to take the time to learn to write in English.

The phone rang.

"Roger," she said.

"You know the address?" he asked.

"Yes, I memorized it when Alina told me a few months ago. That's how I found him."

Klara gave Roger the address to Trevor's house. She waited while he wrote it down. "You have it?"

"Yes."

"Good. Perfect. Trevor's out now. He went to play cards at some man's house."

"What time do you expect him to be back?" Roger asked.

"I don't know for sure. He told me not to prepare his dinner."

"Don't worry your pretty little head about this. I'll have a friend outside waiting for him. I'll make it look like a robbery. You just get yourself out of there. Don't leave anything behind. Make sure. Nothing, don't leave nothing behind. No trace of you ever having been there. Got it?"

"Yes…" Klara stammered. "I think so."

"Good. I'll see you next week. Meet me next Saturday at Mickey's bar at nine p.m. Will you be there?"

"You know I will," Klara said. She hung up the phone and raced into the bathroom, where she got into the tub and scrubbed the shoe polish out of her hair with strong laundry soap. Then she scoured the tub until there was no trace of the brown coloring. Next, she put a scarf around her head. After a quick look in the mirror, she grabbed her handbag, in which she carried a change of clothes. She slipped on her coat. Klara cracked the back door open and looked both ways. She saw no one, so she quietly left the house.

With her head down and her gaze cast to the sidewalk in front of her, she walked as quickly as she could without drawing any attention to herself. When she saw the entrance to the subway station, she ducked inside and raced down the stairs. A quick look around, she spotted the women's bathroom. She walked inside and went immediately into a stall. After locking the door, she changed her clothes. By now, her hair was dry. She wrapped her scarlet tresses into a loose French knot, secured with a comb. After taking a few minutes to put on lipstick and mascara, Klara left the bathroom. She bore no trace of the mousy-brown-haired, nondescript girl who'd worked for Trevor. Klara looked like herself again. When the train came, she returned to the hospital, where she knew she would find Alina with Joey.

twenty-nine
Gilde

London
November 1945

WILLIAM HAD BEEN HOME for two weeks. Gilde knew she should be happier, but somehow, it seemed that the young, innocent girl who'd married William no longer existed.

William had changed, too. When he was not quiet and introspective, he was rambling on about how terrible the POW camp had been for him. He relived the misery daily. And it drove Gilde insane. Gilde could see that he was traumatized, and she'd tried to break through to him. But he was not willing to let her in. The war had taken his passion for life. All of his ideals and his wild romantic exuberance were gone. Several times, she took him in her arms and kissed him passionately. But William didn't respond. He just stood there. He never even kissed her back.

When she met William, she was just a child still living with the Kendall family. At first, she and Jane, the Kendall girl, were best friends, like sisters, but then a boy named Thomas came between them. He had liked Gilde, and although Gilde was not interested in him, Jane never forgave her. From then on, Jane became distant, and then she went to school for nursing training.

Gilde was still living with the Kendalls, but it wasn't the same without Jane. She'd met William the night she'd been on her way home from an acting class when suddenly the city was under siege. Gilde was terrified and froze, unable to run. William's father had pulled her to safety through a tunnel that led to an opening beneath William's family-owned jewelry store as the bombs blasted through the city. Once underground, she recognized Sharon, William's sister, as one of her classmates. It was then that she learned that Sharon's family was Jewish. They accepted her as soon as she declared that she, too, was a Jew.

The next day, she returned to the Kendall home to find the bodies of everyone in the family except Jane. She was only fourteen and had been lost without the Kendalls. Though a classmate's family was willing to take her in temporarily, they made it clear that she wasn't wanted.

Gilde didn't know where to turn. Then she remembered Sharon's family and decided to go back to the jewelry store to see if they would take her in. They opened their home and hearts to her. Their son, William, was young, handsome, and filled with ideals, and she had been attracted to his passion to join the navy and fight against the Nazis. His dream to rid the world of the evil Third Reich was contagious. Even though Gilde didn't want him to leave her and go off to war, she was intoxicated by his commitment. And so, they were married. They spent a few blissful days together, and off he went for training.

When he'd returned on leave, they had a wildly romantic time that left Gilde hopelessly infatuated. But the truth was, she hardly knew him. When the letter came stating that he was missing in action and presumed dead, she'd been forced to go on with her life.

It had been difficult to explain everything that had happened and why she'd done the things she did while William was gone. William listened, but he said nothing; she couldn't tell what he was thinking or feeling.

He'd been gone so long, and so much had changed. She told him about Vicky and her marriage to Alden. She saw the shock on his face, but he said nothing. She went on to tell him about her shameful relationship with Archie. And again, William said nothing.

He never condemned her for her affair with Archie. However, he showed no interest in Vicky either. He never picked her up or played with her. William treated her like something that belonged to Gilde, something he was stuck with but had no feelings for.

His time away and his service in the navy had changed him, too. Gilde learned from him that he had been captured and spent much of the war in a POW camp. The young, idealistic boy he'd been was now a quiet, introspective man. Where he'd once been easy with loving words and physical affection, he was now guarded.

Sometimes, he awoke in the middle of the night, and Gilde would hear him weeping or moaning softly. Then, he would leave the apartment and be gone for hours. Sometimes, he would not return until the following afternoon. If Gilde asked him where he'd been, he would just shake his head, go into the bedroom, and shut the door, locking it behind him. She would be left staring at the door and knowing there was a part of him that he refused to share with her. She wondered if she could ever reach him and help him destroy the demons that haunted him.

Gilde was depressed. She had lost her drive. She'd lost her love of her work, so she did not return to the theater. And the fickle lover, the entertainment world, quickly forgot her.

When William first returned, they attempted to make love, but he could not. After several unsuccessful attempts, William shied away from any physical contact. It embarrassed him that he could not achieve an erection. And Gilde had no idea what to say or do to make it better. So, they didn't discuss it at all.

Then, one night, after having been gone for two consecutive days, William came home filthy drunk. It was very late. Vicky was sleeping, and Gilde had drifted off on the sofa while reading a book. She awakened to hear William whimpering softly as he sat at the kitchen table alone. She could hear him talking to someone from where she lay, but she could hear no other voice. Shaking herself fully awake, she got up and went into the kitchen.

"William? Are you all right?" she asked. His head was in his hands as he rambled incoherently.

"I can't get it out of my mind, the battle. The raid on Dieppe. It was terrible. My friends were dropping all around me, just like that. One minute, they were alive. The next, they were dead. It's very strange how one fights for life. You know what I am trying to say? We were on the beach. I had moments of clarity. My God, Gilde, there was blood, so much blood. But for a second, I'd think, well, maybe the men who died were better off. Because I knew. I mean, I knew I'd be taken prisoner if I lived. But something inside of me wouldn't let me stop fighting. I kept fighting, Gilde. Praying to live, even when I knew that it would be worse to live than to die. Do you understand?"

She nodded. But she didn't completely understand. All she knew was that William was suffering from a terrible internal battle.

"We were trying to take the beach when we were attacked by the German bombers. My God, Gilde, my God," he whispered.

She tried to comfort him by rubbing his shoulders, but he shook her off.

"Gilde, I must tell you something," he said. He was weeping now. His face was wet with tears and snot. His entire body was shaking. His hands lay on his lap, trembling as if they had a life of their own. "Gilde, I shot a man, a young chap, in my own outfit. A friend of mine. A nice fellow. It was an accident. But I killed him. I got nervous, and I shot and killed the poor fellow. My bullet hit him right in the chest. I held him while he bled. We were being attacked. He jumped out in front of me. I killed him, Gilde, I killed him. He and his wife had twins, a boy and a girl. I'd seen their photographs. You see, things were happening so damn fast. It's no excuse, but the truth is that I was so scared that I lost control. Then, as he was dying, I wept. I knew it was my fault. But I couldn't stop it. He was going to die. Oh God, Gilde, I never told anybody about it. No one knows it was me that ended his life. But he haunts me every minute of every day. I killed him. If it weren't for me, he would be alive, at home with his wife and children."

"You don't know that for sure. William. You didn't mean it."

"It doesn't matter if I meant it or not. The end was the same. He's dead and gone."

"I'm so sorry," she said, taking his cold hand in hers.

"Do you know where hell is?"

She shook her head, not knowing what to say to him.

"It's a POW camp. The Nazi sons of bitches threw me and the others that were still alive from my crew on a train and took us to a POW camp that they called Marlag. The train ride was hot and crowded, but at least every so often, they stopped and let us take a piss. I would have tried to escape. I thought about it. In fact, I looked for every possible way to do it. But it wasn't possible. We were well outnumbered, and they had their guns pointed right at us, smiling all the while like they were just hoping one of us would run so they could use the poor bastard as an example of what would happen if we ever tried to get out. Then they threw us in this miserable camp that they built to keep and torture prisoners. But you know how I am. I couldn't just take it lying down, not me. So I talked to the guy in the bunk above mine. He and I decided to try and devise a way to escape."

His hand had tensed around Gilde's hand. He was squeezing tightly. It felt like her fingers were being crushed. She longed to take her hand away, but she didn't want to stop him from talking. William's face was blood red, and he was shaking.

"Escape?" he went on. "Impossible. I mean, I thought of everything. I couldn't sleep. That's how fixated I was on finding a way. But, when I say it wasn't possible, I mean it wasn't. The entire place was surrounded by barbed wire. The prisoners were starving. We were so hungry we were eating rats and bugs. I never knew what hunger was until I got into that hellhole, and during the winter, the rooms where they kept us were freezing. My eyes were constantly tearing from the cold, and then, would you believe, tiny icicles formed on my eyelashes. It was worse than you can possibly imagine.

"And they were inhuman. We'd ask them for blankets, and they'd just laugh. It was like they had no feelings at all. But, thank God, at least there was a charcoal stove burning in the middle of the room, and all of us guys would sleep in a circle around it on the nights that it was so frigid we couldn't stop shaking. The damn thing stank, and the smoke from it made it hard to breathe. I was coughing up black mucus all night. But we were glad to have it. I think we might have all frozen to death if we didn't. You know, they knew that they weren't supposed to torture us according to the Geneva Convention."

"No, they weren't," she said helplessly.

"But they did. Boy, oh boy, did they. A couple of my buddies died from the torture. A few others died from starvation. I ask myself every day why I was spared. I can't enjoy anything. I feel too guilty for having lived and for what I did … God, Gilde, what I did to that poor guy. I know it was an accident, but it doesn't matter. The point is he's dead. He'll never see his family again … never hold his wife, never see his children get married. Do you understand how that weighs on me? Then when I got back to London, I went right home, looking for my family and for you. "

"Oh, William, I am so sorry," Gilde said. She was crying.

"That's when I found out that my mother died from a heart attack. I can't help but ask myself if I might have caused her to get sick because I joined the service. First my dad, then my mum. Did my choices in life kill them? Maybe they did," he said in a hoarse voice, shrugging. But Gilde could see the tears forming in his eyes.

"No, Will. You are not responsible for their deaths. You went to war because you felt you had to. It was noble. You did what you thought was right. The war had to be fought, Hitler had to be defeated, or he would have conquered the world, and can you imagine what would have happened then?" She reached up and touched his face. "Will, you followed your heart. You gave your life over to a cause you believed in."

"I don't know, Gilde. I just don't know. I close my eyes at night, and I see the bombs exploding and the bodies flying like rag dolls, lifeless in a macabre ballet in midair in my mind." He started to weep. "It's hard to admit this, but I was afraid, Gilde. The truth is I am a coward. I was afraid. I am still afraid."

"I can understand your being afraid when you were at war. But why now, Will? What are you afraid of now? The war is over. You're safe here in London with me. Let's try to start our lives over. We're both still young. Please give yourself a chance. Give us a chance." She took his hand. He allowed her to hold it for a few minutes. "Will you come to bed with me? Will you just lie in my arms and allow me to hold you for a little while?"

He nodded. "Yes…"

"Oh, Will, maybe we really can start over? Maybe we can find what we had together before you left and begin to rebuild on that foundation. Are you willing to try with me?" she asked, tears clouding her eyes as she remembered their wedding day.

They'd had so little time together before and after their marriage, and even now. But before William had gone off to war, there had been a sweet and innocent love between them.

Maybe they could find that feeling again, and then perhaps he might return to her as the man he once was. She had made so many mistakes in her life. She had so many regrets. In fact, even when William had first returned, even before she knew how damaged he was, she was thinking about the mistakes she'd made with Alden and how she was sorry for the things she'd done to destroy their beautiful marriage.

Then, when William returned, she thought he might be just what she needed. After all, Alden was gone. And, once, she and William had been deeply in love. But William wasn't the same man. He had come back in body, but his heart and mind were distant and so different from before that she had no idea how to start over with him. Could this conversation be the beginning of a second chance for them as a couple? Gilde whispered a prayer, asking God to lead her to happiness.

"I hope you can forgive me for everything I did when I thought you were dead?"

"You mean the affair, the baby, and your second marriage?"

"Yes, Will, that's what I mean. I have to know that you forgive me if we are going to try to make it work between us, because I can't change the past."

He squeezed her hand. "I can't really blame you for anything. You thought I was dead. You were all alone. You did the best you could."

Now, she couldn't hold back the tears, and Gilde began to weep. His forgiveness made her feel so sorry for everything that had hurt him and hopeful about the future.

"Let me clean up a little." He smiled. "I hate to admit it, but I'm a drunk. I don't want to come to bed with you like this. I am a stinking mess."

She smiled back at him.

"I'll pull myself together and meet you in the bedroom. What do you say?" he said, touching her cheek.

Gilde nodded. He looked like the old William. The man she'd fallen in love with. Her heart was beating fast, and her face was still wet with tears.

He reached up and gently wiped a tear from her face with his thumb. William looked into her eyes and smiled. "Gilde, Gilde..." he whispered. Then he got up and went to the back of the apartment, and she heard the bathroom door close softly.

Quickly, Gilde rushed to the bedroom to change into a silk negligee that she hoped he would find enticing. It had been a while since she'd worn it, actually since Alden had left. She rummaged through everything in her drawers until she saw the black silk. When she did, she pulled the gown out and laid it on her bed. It was quite beautiful.

The gown had a deep neckline of black lace that showed off her lovely white cleavage. It fit her form perfectly, not too tight or too loose. Carefully, she removed her silk stockings. She'd acquired several pairs since she'd begun her work on the stage. But they were expensive, and she always took care not to run them. She stood, holding one of the stockings for a moment, and remembered when William gave her her first pair as a gift. How excited she'd been to have such a coveted item. And how pleased he'd been with himself to be able to acquire the stockings and give them to her. She remembered his broad smile and his bright eyes. If, by some miracle, they could find a way back to that feeling, the feeling they'd shared that day. Then, as Gilde unbuttoned her blouse, the entire room trembled with the crash of a roaring gunshot.

"William! No, no…" she fell to her knees. But she already knew it was too late.

thirty

Gilde

NOT MANY PEOPLE attended William's funeral. After the war and the bombing, there were not many old friends left. Only Sharon and Gilde stood at the gravesite. And because so much time had elapsed and so much had happened since the last time Sharon and Gilde had seen each other, their conversation was strained and awkward. It wasn't so much the time apart that made them both ill at ease as it was the way that William died. Gilde didn't want to explain anything about William's last hours and was glad Sharon hadn't asked. Vicky refused to stay in her buggy. She wanted Gilde to hold her. The child was crabby all day, crying on and off as if she had an antenna, and was miserable in reaction to what her mother was feeling.

Sharon walked over to Gilde and awkwardly kissed her cheek. Neither said much.

It was obvious to Gilde that Sharon felt as uneasy as she did, and Gilde wasn't surprised when Sharon told her that she had to leave. "I'm sorry, I can't come by for the shiva. I have to go to work. It's mandatory, I'm afraid," Sharon said.

Gilde doubted that Sharon was telling her the truth. After all, her brother died. Gilde was sure Sharon could have gotten the day off if she had gone to her boss. But truth be told, Gilde was glad Sharon was leaving.

They said a quick and uncomfortable goodbye at the cemetery. There would be no shiva. Gilde hadn't followed the Jewish religion for many years. She had not changed her religion, but she didn't observe Jewish laws. And so, she would have felt like a hypocrite if she had tried to follow Jewish customs. Besides, there was no one to sit shiva with, and she didn't know ten Jewish men with whom she could ask to have a minyan for her husband. It had been years since she'd been to a synagogue or talked to a rabbi, so she couldn't ask for help there.

Her heart was aching, so instead of going home and covering the mirrors, taking off her shoes, and sitting on a hard box alone in the house with just her child, Gilde walked along the tree-lined streets, looking around and feeling lost.

The motion of the buggy put Vicky to sleep, and she was glad for the peace. After an hour of walking, Vicky awoke hungry and still crabby. Gilde took her home. She fed Vicky. Then, by some miracle, maybe the fresh air, Vicky napped.

Now that she was alone, Gilde had to face the truth. She had to clean up the mess that was all she had left of her husband. Gilde got on her hands and knees, and with wet rags, she scrubbed the blood and bits of the brain off the bathroom floor and walls. Several times, she gagged, and once, she vomited. When the room was clean, she washed her hands, scouring them until they were raw. Then she sat on the living room sofa and felt sorry for herself. It seemed as if everything in her life had gone wrong. She couldn't find her family and wouldn't even know where to begin, especially since it was almost impossible for her to get to Berlin. Every audition she'd gone on since Alden left had been a failure.

Now, William was truly dead. There was no denying it.

She'd been hopeful when he'd come back unexpectedly. But the man who returned was not the same William she'd married so long ago, and the man who died in her bathroom was a man she hardly knew.

Still, the horror of his suicide had shaken her to the very core, and she wondered if there was anything, anything at all, she could have done to prevent it.

Then there was Alden. She was hurting inside, but the pain of losing Alden was the greatest pain of all. Dear Alden, her best friend, her one true love, and her solid oak tree, the only person she felt she could lean on, was gone.

She had a little money saved, but it wouldn't last long. She had to go back to work. But what could she do? Because she'd fallen pregnant, she'd been unable to finish her training. She could no longer afford to pay a nanny to help with Vicky. Therefore, she could not return to her nursing training because she couldn't leave her daughter alone while working at a hospital.

Without the theater, Gilde had absolutely no source of income. She had lost her pension years ago. Once William was presumed dead, the navy cut off all of her allowances. So, she needed to find a way to earn enough money to survive. Gilde had put away a small amount of savings, but it wouldn't last forever. Now, she not only had herself to think of, but she also had to take care of Vicky. A job, she needed some kind of job.

She was racking her brain. It would probably be good for her to occupy her time. Sitting at home alone with a small child all day without any purpose would surely drive her insane. She knew that if she did that, she would obsess about Alden. So, she needed to figure out the kind of work that would allow her to keep Vicky with her.

Gilde bit her lower lip. The apartment where she lived was large enough for her to start school. An acting, singing, and dancing school for children. She had the background. Even if she had never really made it big on the London stage, she still had enough of a resume to attract parents with dreams of stardom for their children. And if she worked it all out properly, she could keep Vicky with her while she taught. Perhaps even have someone come in to help with Vicky for an hour or two. It would be much less expensive than a full-time nurse.

Gilde shrugged. Why not? It would give her an outlet for the art she loved and an opportunity to help children who loved the theater as much as she did. With God's help, if she could get enough students, she would be able to afford to stay in this flat. If not, she'd find something smaller.

thirty-one
Gilde

THE CHILDREN'S acting school didn't start off with a bang. Gilde's short moments of fame were not enough to generate great interest and a huge influx of students. Still, the students who did sign up were children of well-to-do parents willing to make donations to support the arts. They were excited about seeing their children in productions, even if they were only performed on a makeshift stage in Gilde's large living room. And so *Gilde Thornbury's School for the Performing Arts* began.

The parents of students recommended the classes to friends. Before she knew it, Gilde had ten dedicated students, seven girls and three boys, all pre-teens. It was fun and rewarding for Gilde to watch them grow in the craft she loved. But after Vicky went to bed at night, she was terribly lonely, and her thoughts always turned to Alden. She wondered how he was doing. If he ever thought about her, if he ever remembered the good times they shared.

Because of Alden's love for Christmas, Gilde had come to love the spirit of the holiday, too. It was only a week until Christmas, and she wanted to buy small gifts for each student. Alden had shown her the joy of giving. Each Christmas, the two of them went out and purchased small gifts for their coworkers, and sometimes, when they could afford to, they bought small gifts of food for the poor. Shopping for little presents for her students, whom she adored, would make her feel good, Gilde decided. So, she dressed Vicky warmly and took her in a taxi to Harrods. The store was decorated for Christmas.

Harrods' Christmas decorations were not nearly as elaborate as they had been before the war, but the most festive it had been since. However, instead of making Gilde feel warm and joyful, the holiday atmosphere left her empty and alone. She thought she would enjoy walking through the store all day and making selections. Instead, she found that she wanted to hurry, buy her gifts, and go home.

It was noon when Gilde finished. She was hungry, famished, in fact. *I should have had something for breakfast*, she thought. But it had been almost a week since she'd gone food shopping, and she had nothing to eat in the apartment except for Vicky's cereals and milk. So, after Gilde made her purchases, she and Vicky stopped at the restaurant inside Harrods for a quick lunch.

A woman sat alone just a few tables from where Gilde was seated. There was something terribly familiar about the woman. In fact, Gilde couldn't help but stare. All she could see was the side of the woman's face. The way her hair fell across the nape of her neck. The way she moved her hand to push the hair back from her face, how she crossed her legs. And the way she held her fork. There was no mistaking this woman; it was undeniable, and yes, she was older, but it was Jane. Gilde felt like she might vomit. They would be face to face if Jane turned even the slightest bit. So many different emotions came rushing like the rapids in a river.

Once, long ago, Jane had been her best friend, her savior. When she first came to London on the Kindertransport, it was Jane who had taken her under her wing. Jane had forced the other girls in school to accept Gilde. Jane's parents had taken Gilde into their home and treated her with the utmost kindness.

Then Thomas ruined everything. He was the most handsome boy in school, and Jane was crazy about him. Every night, she told Gilde how she felt. So, when Thomas declared his love for Gilde, Gilde was sick with fear. She rejected Thomas but could not bring herself to tell

Jane what had happened. Then, when war broke out, and Thomas was leaving for the army, he took it upon himself to tell Jane how he felt about Gilde. From that day on, everything changed between Jane and Gilde. It didn't matter that Gilde had no interest in Thomas.

The bond between the two girls gradually faded away, leaving Jane completely disconnected from the friendship. It broke Gilde's heart. They had been best friends, sharing everything. But that was over, and Jane never even told Gilde when she decided to go for nurse training. Instead, she announced her plans to the family at the dinner table one night. Then, just like that, she was gone.

Gilde had never felt so lost. She wished that she and Jane could be close again, like sisters, and that they could comfort each other. But that never happened. Gilde had not been in communication with Jane. It had been years since she'd even heard Jane's name.

Then, Alden had brought Jane back into her life. But not in the way she would have wished for. Her beloved husband Alden had left her for Jane, her once dearest friend… The betrayal had hurt more than she could have ever imagined. Gilde still couldn't believe the affair between Alden and Jane had snuck up on her. She had no idea what was going on until it was too late. Jane was a nurse working with Alden, giving him the time and attention that Gilde had forgotten to shower on her husband when she began her career in the theater. It wasn't that she'd ever stopped loving Alden. She'd just gotten caught up and took his love for granted. A terrible mistake, she thought.

"Gilde…" Jane said.

Gilde forced a smile. "It's been a long time," she said.

"No sense in trying to have a conversation from across the room. May I join you?" Jane asked.

Was she serious? Gilde was caught off guard. She owed Jane so much, but she was still angry and hurt. "Yes, of course," Gilde said, not knowing what else to do.

As Jane got up and walked over to sit down at Gilde's table, Gilde couldn't help but think about Jane and Alden making love. Her stomach was turning. Before she sat down, Jane leaned over and looked into Vicky's buggy. Vicky had fallen asleep.

"She's beautiful. Alden said she was beautiful," Jane said. *How is she so calm? It's unnerving,* Gilde thought. The mention of Alden's name sent a shiver up Gilde's spine.

Jane sat across from her. The memories of giggling in bed until the wee hours of the morning when they were just children kept coming back to Gilde. The sadness of loss was overwhelming.

A young waitress with a bright smile, pen and paper in hand, walked over. "Can I take your order?" Gilde had lost her appetite. "Tea, please," she told the waitress.

"I'll have the same," Jane replied. "And an order of fish and chips."

The waitress walked away, and an awkward silence fell like a fog between them.

"I miss the beauty of Christmas the way it was before the war," Jane said wistfully.

Gilde could hardly breathe. She wanted to say so much but could not find a beginning or an end. Her feelings were so jumbled. This was Jane sitting across from her. The closest friend she'd ever had and the toughest betrayal and enemy she'd ever known.

"He was my husband…" Gilde finally whimpered. Then she put her head in her hands. There was a strained silence. It seemed like a long time before she began to speak again. "I know I owe you and your family a great deal, but Jane, I, and Alden were married. For God's sake, Jane, he was my husband."

Jane's eyes were shining, and it suddenly became clear to Gilde that Jane was strangely enjoying this. Jane must have wanted to punish Gilde for what she perceived as stealing Thomas from her. That wasn't the way it really happened. Gilde didn't take him from her. She would never have done that. But that wasn't how Jane saw it. And now, Gilde could see the triumph on Jane's face.

"When Alden and I met, we became friends. He had so much time on his hands he was working extra shifts so as not to be home alone taking care of the baby. It must have been convenient for you, I mean, Alden, taking care of your child so you can selfishly pursue your grand attempt at stardom. Let's face it, Gilde, you were busy. You were always all show and glamour, weren't you?"

"No, Jane, I was a shy young girl, innocent, foreign when I met you. You were my best friend. You were…"

"And you went behind my back and used your big breasts and sexy little ways to seduce Thomas."

"No, Jane. No, that's not what happened. Not at all."

"Well, it's how things ended up, isn't it? Anyway, as far as you and Alden and this marriage… Gilde, you were on your way to becoming a famous actress. It seemed to me that you had lost interest in him, in being a wife to him. Alden and I got along. We have a lot in common."

"Jane? You don't understand. I loved him. I really loved him. I just got caught up."

"The way I once loved Thomas?"

"I can't believe you are still holding that against me after all these years. I swear to you, I never encouraged Thomas."

"You ruined my life. I loved you and made you my best friend. You came to Britain without any friends or family, with no money, with nothing. It was me who stood up for you when everyone turned their back on you. My family housed you and fed you when we barely had enough food ourselves. But what we had we shared with you. Then you turned on me and took the only man I loved. You knew how I felt about him. I told you in confidence. We talked about him every night. You knew he was the man I wanted to marry, Gilde."

"I never took him, Jane. I never wanted him."

"Be serious, Gilde. I've played this over in my mind for years. Something happened that night when we went to the dance. You were with that boy. I can't remember his name. I was with Thomas. And you knew how I felt about Thomas. But then Thomas danced with you, and after that dance, everything between Thomas and me changed. I don't know what you said. I don't know if you promised him something and then began meeting him secretly. All I know is that you had to do something to encourage his feelings, or he could not have fallen so hard for you. I hated you then, Gilde. All the love I had for you turned to hate."

The waitress put the cups down on the table. Neither Gilde nor Jane touched their tea.

"So, you met Alden, and when you found out he was married to me, you decided to take him away from me to punish me for Thomas."

"Sort of. I suppose so. Actually, yes, exactly. But don't try to tell that to Alden. I'll deny every word of it, and you will only look like a jealous, foolish woman."

"Oh Jane, my God. Do you care about him at all?"

"I love him now. I've gotten to know what a wonderful man he is, and I love him. I am pregnant with his child."

"The ink isn't even dry on my divorce papers, and already you are having a baby."

"We got married the day the divorce was finalized."

"If you wanted to hurt me, you succeeded," Gilde said.

"Yes, well, I had to get pregnant. At first, he missed Vicky like crazy. I was afraid he'd go back to you just to see the child. I know she's not his. He told me. But he loved her. Now he will have his own, and he'll forget you and Vicky."

"And so you have your revenge, Jane. It may mean nothing to you, but I want you to know that I never did anything to hurt you with Thomas. Never. And I loved you, Jane. You were my best friend, my sister. I loved your family and appreciated them beyond measure. And because I loved you so much, the hurt that I am feeling now is so much deeper than it would have been if this had happened with a stranger. There is nothing I can say or do to change anything. I made a mistake. I was star-struck for a while and lost my way. But you needn't worry. I won't come looking for Alden. He is happy with you. You say that you love him. I want him to be happy because I love him too. For years, years, Jane, I missed you, I loved you. I wished I could somehow find you and make things right between us. But you win, you've succeeded. I don't love you anymore."

Gilde stood up, straightened her back, and lifted her chin. Then she put her arms through her overcoat. Her hands trembled as she went into her handbag and took a few coins, dropping them on the table to cover the bill. Then, without saying another word to Jane, she picked up her shopping bag and pushed Vicky's pram out of the restaurant.

Then, still trembling, she got on the elevator. "What floor, Ma'am," the elevator operator asked.

"Ground floor, please."

The elevator door opened to a store filled with holiday shoppers. This trip made Gilde feel worse than she did before she left. She was hoping it would brighten her spirits; instead, she saw, of all people, Jane.

A quick glance into the buggy reassured Gilde that Vicky was still sleeping. She put Vicky's coat and hat on, trying not to disturb her. Vicky was groggy from all the morning's excitement, so she lay down and fell back to sleep. *I'll feed her when we get home.* Then she put a heavy blanket over her daughter and kept walking until she left the department store.

A light dusting of snow covered the sidewalk. Large, powdery flakes fell into Gilde's hair and mingled with the tears that stung her cheeks. She overheard a man and woman talking. They said something about the snow looking like it would turn into a winter storm, but she didn't care. All she knew was that she wanted to get home, as far away from Harrods as possible. She was glad she'd purchased some food before she had seen Jane. It would hold her and Vicky over for a few days. Later in the week, she'd call a babysitter to come over for a few hours so she could go out and shop for food.

"Taxi," Gilde walked close to the curb, still holding tight to Vicky's pram. Then she raised her hand. A young cabbie maneuvered his car over to pick up the fare. Gilde held Vicky in her arms while the cabbie put Vicky's buggy into the car. It was a relief to hide her tears in the cab's backseat. She was glad to be leaving the Knightsbridge area before someone recognized her and asked her for an autograph. All she wanted right now was to be alone.

thirty-two
Alden

December 1945

DR. ALDEN THORNBURY sat by himself in the doctors' dining room. He had been working since early that morning without a break and had finally stopped to grab a quick meal in the cafeteria. He watched the snow falling outside the window.

What had started as a light dusting earlier that morning was now turning into a storm. He was concerned because Jane, his wife, had taken the day off work to go to Harrods to do her Christmas shopping. She was pregnant, and he was concerned about her being out in this weather. The temperature had dropped, and therefore, there would be frozen patches of ice hidden beneath the snow. She might slip and fall. Anything could happen.

When did I become such a nervous man? Alden shook his head. He loved Jane and was happy and excited that he was about to be the father of his first biological child. Jane was a good wife and a good friend. She never complained about his long work hours and always made sure she had food ready when he came home. Yes, he loved her.

But he wasn't madly in love with her. Not the way he'd been with Gilde. Alden had tried many times to recreate the passion and intensity of emotion he had for Gilde with Jane, but it wasn't possible. In fact, he couldn't help but think or dream about Gilde.

He could still remember how he shivered when Gilde's long golden curls fell on his chest after they made love. Gilde. She was like a bright shooting star that had come into his life and illuminated it until it was as bright as the sun. For a short while, he believed he'd been able to make her happy. His love for her was so intense that it made his heart feel like it might explode, and for a while, it had been enough.

But then, she was too bright, too sparkling for the life he offered. The stage swept her away from him. Then he knew. He knew he'd lost her from the first time he saw her perform and watched as the audience went wild. Oh, he believed that she loved him. But Gilde was bigger than that love. Her light encompassed the world. That was obvious by how the audience stood up, applauding madly as soon as she took her bow. The day finally came when he had to face the fact that even though he loved her, she was better off without him. If he'd stayed with her, he would have held her back. That would have been selfish. And he cared too much about her happiness to be selfish.

Gilde didn't call him when she received the divorce papers. In fact, she'd signed them quickly. A part of him hoped she would contact him and beg him to come home, even though he felt he was doing what was best for her. Still, when the divorce was finalized, Alden had been devastated, but Jane was there—caring, gentle, and loving Jane. They would make a life together. She promised him he would be happy. She was a nurse, so she understood that as a doctor, he would be expected to work long hours and be called in to work on a case at the last minute. She knew that this was the life of a physician, and she expected no different from him.

Jane was kind to him and compassionate about his failed marriage. She knew he was still in love with Gilde. Alden would never lie to her. But she wanted to marry him anyway. And he knew that he should feel blessed. He should be grateful to have such a wonderful woman as his wife. But his heart and his mind were constantly in battle. His heart longed for Gilde's golden curls. The nights they shared brought him to places of passion he never knew existed while his mind told him: *Jane understands you. She will make you a good wife.*

Stop thinking about the past, about the woman who makes you crazy with desire, or you might go out of your mind, Alden warned himself. *Be grateful for what God has given you, or you might lose what you have.* He was suddenly afraid that a part of him might wish to be rid of Jane. His heart started racing as he watched the blizzard outside the window. If something happened to her in the storm, he would blame himself.

Every few minutes throughout the rest of Alden's work shift, he said prayers for Jane's safety and the well-being of their unborn child. He thought as he stitched a deep cut on a child's finger. *Dear God, I am grateful for all you have given me. Please don't think I don't appreciate your sending me a good and kind woman. Thank you for all you have given me, a wife who is going to have my baby,* he thought as he listened to the heartbeat of an old man.

Finally, his shift was over. It was so cold that the snow hardened on the ground, and more continued falling. Alden was exhausted but couldn't wait to open the door to his flat and be reassured that Jane was all right. He had no idea why he felt so fearful, but he could not shake the trepidation. As he turned the door handle and walked inside, his heart beat so fast that he felt dizzy. It was very early morning. Jane should still be asleep. But she wasn't. The smell of bacon frying filled the small apartment. Jane was alright. She was standing at the stove making his breakfast. *Thank you, God, thank you. Forgive me for my thoughts of Gilde.*

"Tough night?" Jane asked, turning to smile at him, her lipstick drawn on perfectly.

"Yes, a little. I was worried about you in the storm. Did you change your mind about going to Harrods yesterday?"

"No, I went."

"Even in this terrible weather?"

"Yes, dear. But I got home early before the storm got bad."

"I'm so glad you got home safely," he said, hanging his coat on the rack and removing his wool scarf.

Jane smiled at Alden. "Sit down. Your food is ready."

He sat down and began to eat. She watched him lovingly. He was her victory, her husband, and the father of her unborn child. At first, he'd been a prize she'd won, but as they spent time together, she'd realized that she really did love him. As she watched him eating, she knew she would never tell him about her meeting with Gilde that afternoon.

thirty-three

Alina

New York
December 1945

AFTER ALINA WAS CLEARED of any involvement in the murder of Trevor Powell, she received all the money and possessions he'd willed to her. He'd added her to his will when they were first married, and she couldn't believe he hadn't changed his will when she left him.

She wondered why. Either he'd forgotten, or he had somehow hoped she would return. But Trevor was dead, and the answers to those questions died with him. Alina would never know.

When she'd first heard about Trevor's death, she'd been shocked and even horrified. Not that she would miss him. But the very idea that he'd been murdered came as a surprise. A police officer had come to her when she and Klara were staying at Roger's house and began asking questions.

She couldn't believe it, but they were considering her a suspect. He had been out playing cards with friends. According to the others in the card group, they made large bets, so he'd been carrying a lot of money with him. He had been on his way home when he was robbed and shot dead.

When his body was found, each of the other card players had been questioned by the police, but all of them had an alibi. Alina, too, had a very valid alibi. She'd been sitting beside Joey's bed at the hospital, and every nurse and doctor had been more than willing to vouch for her. It was finally concluded that Trevor's murder was a random robbery. The police thought that maybe someone knew of the cash and the card game, but they could not find any suspects. The case was still open but remained unsolved.

Alina and Klara had moved into the home of one of her clients. His name was Roger. Alina hardly remembered him. He had always come and gone from the house so quietly that she hadn't taken much notice. He never sat in the main room with the others.

Roger was a private man, not boisterous like some of the others. However, Roger was kind enough to offer her and Klara a place to stay until Joey was released from the hospital and until Trevor's will was settled. Roger was so kind to Klara that Alina thought he was an angel. He opened his home to them. He made them both comfortable and made sure they wanted for nothing.

Then, once Alina was awarded possession of Trevor's home, Klara and Roger left for a week and went on a short vacation to Grossinger's resort in the Catskills. Joey was released from the hospital, and by mid-December, Alina, Joey, and Klara had moved into Trevor's home in Manhattan.

For the first week, Joey had nightmares that Alina was sure stemmed from his early life in that same house. But as Alina continued to explain to Joey that Trevor had passed away and would never be returning, the child began to relax.

The fire had affected his lungs, and Joey not only had a twisted body but his breathing was labored. He wheezed with every inhale. Alina had a secret and horrible knowing deep inside of her that gnawed at her and made her miserable. She knew that Joey would not live to be an old man, and each day she shared with her son was a gift. The more she thought about this gift, the more she felt compelled to bring Joey to Germany to meet Lotti.

Lotti was his aunt, Johan's sister. She was the only living blood relative on Johan's side of the family that Alina had ever really known. It was only right that she bring the two of them together while Joey was still well enough to make the trip. Since she inherited a small fortune from Trevor, she had the money to travel back to Germany. And, since she no longer owned a brothel, she could feel comfortable meeting with Lotti and her family again. They need never know about the whorehouse, or how she survived the war.

One night, after Joey had fallen asleep, Klara and Alina sat in the kitchen, sipping cups of Trevor's finest coffee.

"Trevor was a true bastard, but still, I can't help but feel bad that his life ended so violently," Alina said.

"Yes, it's terribly sad. But, let's face it, Alina, he was a danger to you and Joey. It is a blessing to have him gone. He could have killed you," Klara said, lighting a cigarette and turning away from Alina.

She would never tell Alina that she was responsible for arranging to have Trevor killed. Alina was better off not knowing anything about what transpired. As long as Alina was ignorant of what Klara had done, Alina need never feel any guilt or responsibility for any of it. And this was what Klara wanted for her dear friend. A happy, healthy life, free of shame and guilt.

"I don't think I want to reopen the house, Klara. But I want to give you enough money so that you can open it if you want to. And of course, you know, you are welcome to stay here at my home, with Joey and me, forever if you'd like."

Klara heaved a sigh. "That's kind of you. But, I think I'd like to open a brothel of my own. I would like to be independent. To have my own income."

"I understand, and I would like to give you the money to open it," Alina said, looking directly into Klara's eyes. "You've been a friend to me, a true friend."

Klara took a long drag on her cigarette. The way Alina said that made Klara wonder if Alina knew what Klara had done to Trevor. But Klara said nothing.

"I want to go to Berlin to try to find my family. I want to see if I can find Johan's sister as well. I think she deserves to meet her nephew," Alina said, taking a cigarette out of the pack and lighting it.

"Are you sure, Alina?"

Alina nodded.

"You don't know what you will find when you return to Germany. The war was brutal."

"I know that, and I'm afraid. But I can't go on without knowing the truth. I must do what I can to find out what happened to all the people from my past. My family, my friends. People who I have loved. It's hard to just forget and let them go."

"So, what will you do? Go to Berlin and go back to your childhood home?"

"No, I don't think it would be that easy, Klara. I will try, but I don't think anyone will be there. My parents and sister were gone before I even left. But, there was this woman. Her name was Lotti, and she was a friend of mine and my family. Her brother was Johan, Joey's father. Lev, her husband, was my father's business partner. Their address is the last known address I have. Before I left Germany, my family's house and business were already confiscated by the Nazis. It would be of no use to even try to start there."

"Confiscated?"

"Yes, taken away and given to a German non-Jewish family on Kristallnacht. Stolen," Alina said. "It's a very long story, but my parents were arrested, and my sister went to a safe family in London. At least, I hope she is safe. I don't know. I am hoping that Lotti and Lev will know where to find them."

"So, you have their address?"

"Yes, of course. I could never forget it. I know their phone number, too."

"Should we write or try to call?" Klara said.

The thought of calling made Alina's heart race. It was difficult to make any long-distance call from the United States to overseas, but it was almost impossible to reach Berlin with the system so damaged. Then, if by some miracle the operator was able to get through, what if Lotti or Lev didn't answer? What then? She couldn't bear it.

They were her last hope of ever finding her family. If Lotti or Lev didn't answer or the phone was disconnected, she honestly had nowhere else to look. "Write, yes, I'll write. That's what I'll do." If she wrote, she could always try to call in the future. But at least she wouldn't have to know any absolute truths immediately.

"I'll help you," Klara said.

"No, I have to do this alone. Please don't be offended," Alina said.

"I'm not offended. That's what I like about our friendship. Neither of us pushes the other to do uncomfortable things. I understand you, Alina," Klara said.

thirty-four

Alina

ALINA WROTE and rewrote the letter several times, tearing it up and starting over. There was so much she wanted to say, and yet so much she couldn't. Once, she even decided to try to call. But when she lifted the black telephone receiver and held it against her chest, she was terrified. For several moments, her mind went blank. How could she forget Lotti's number? Alina's breathing was shallow. Her heart was beating so hard that she felt nauseated and dizzy, and her head ached. Her hand trembled as she replaced the phone receiver on the handset. A phone call would be too final, too difficult; the fear of a possible immediate answer to the unknown was too trying on her nerves.

With a call, all the answers to all of her pressing questions might be revealed instantly. And the answers, dear God, the answers could be devastating. No, she couldn't bear to dial the number. The emotions were too intense. She would try to write again. Yes, that's what she would do, and if, God forbid, there was no answer to her letter, then she would place the dreaded telephone call.

Her slender fingers trembled as she held the pen in her hand. Then she began to write the letter once again. And once again, but in different words, she asked the same questions she'd asked in every other letter she'd torn up and discarded. However, Alina knew that her fears had nothing to do with the wording of the letter. She had avoided opening this door to the past for such a long time and was terrified of what she might discover. After all that had happened during the war, there was a damn good possibility that they were all dead. Her parents, Lotti, Lev, and even Gilde. Dead, gone forever. Very possible.

Was it better to know the truth or live safely in darkness forever? It was a Pandora's box that was sitting before her, represented by the paper and pen that lay on the table. Best to keep that box shut tight. Best to live only with the memories? Easier for sure, and yet, she could not leave it alone. She must know the truth. Finally, she had to lift the lid and see what lay inside the box.

These people were her blood. They all deserved to know Joey, and he to know them. He had grandparents and an aunt somewhere on the other side of the world. They might no longer be alive, but then again … they might. A tear held to her eyelashes as she tapped the pen against her lips.

Then, a memory brought a wry smile to her face. Alina remembered how Otto, her mother's lover, had once told her and Bridget the story of Pandora's box. She had remembered the box, but she'd forgotten the end. Now, she remembered, and it was as if a flicker of light was lit in her soul. Wasn't hope the last thing that came out of Pandora's box?

She whispered the word aloud, "hope," tasting the letters and the meaning as she rolled it around in her mouth. *I must have hope. I can't lose sight of hope. I will keep it lit like a candle flame. Yes, hope. I can feel that flicker of light in my heart.* She bit her lower lip. When she picked up the pen and began writing again in German, she knew she would not discard this letter. This letter will be sent.

Dear Lotti,

It's Alina. I hope this letter finds you and Lev doing well. I don't even know if you will ever receive this correspondence because I am not sure how well the mail is getting through from America to Berlin. But I must try. In truth, I can't even be sure that you are still at the same address. But if you do by God's grace, get this letter, and I pray that you do, please know that I love you. I am now living in the City of New York, America. It is a very long story of how I got here. For now, please know that I am healthy and doing fine. Have you seen or heard from my parents or my sister? I miss all of you so much. I think of you often. Lotti, there is so much I must tell you. But I cannot tell you all of it in a letter. I do think that you should know that you have a nephew. Johan and I have a son. His name is Joseph, but I call him Joey. I know you will love him. He is the light of my life, Lotti, and I can't wait for you to meet him. If it is alright with you, I think it is best that I come to Berlin and see you and talk to you in person. Please answer and let me know if you would like me to come. I won't come until I receive word from you that you want to see me.

With love, your sister through friendship,

Alina

Alina didn't have the heart to tell Lotti about Johan's death. Not in a letter. Alina knew how hard Lotti would take it, especially since they had fought the last time Lotti and Johan had spoken. It was best to soften the blow by telling her in person.

Alina sealed the letter and then walked to the post office. She could easily afford a taxi but wanted to feel the cold, sobering wind on her skin. Once this letter left her hands and was on its way to Berlin, everything would be set into motion. She would cast her hope into the wind and wait for an answer. Her stomach felt a little nervous, but she was not going to change her mind. She pulled her coat more tightly around her slender figure. A little voice in her mind said there was still time to turn back. But she didn't. With her head high and hair billowing in the wind, she walked into the post office, paid the postage, and watched the letter drop into the outgoing mailbag. Then she stepped outside.

Now, she would hail a cab and head home. As soon as she got back, she'd have a nice cup of hot tea and maybe add a bit of brandy. Right now, she needed something to calm her nerves. She walked towards the street and tried to stop a taxi, but they were all full. Then a car went by, driving too fast for the crowded street, its wheels splashing her with dirty slush. Damn, she whispered as she looked down at her coat. It was a lovely ivory wool. Klara warned her when she bought it that it would surely attract plenty of dirt because it was such a light color. Well, Klara, she thought, you were right. The coat was full of gray slush. She should have been upset, but instead, she wanted to laugh. Somehow, sending that letter had lightened the burden in her heart. It was just a coat. For a moment, she forgot that she had plenty of money to buy another one.

Then she heard a familiar male voice call her name.

"Alina?"

She turned around quickly, and there was Ugo. A smile broke out on her face and in her heart. The smile reached from her lips to her eyes. The joy she felt at seeing him was as natural as breathing. He came towards her. There was a slight drag on his left leg and a deep scar under his left eye. He looked older; his hair had streaks of gray, but he was Ugo, still Ugo, and more importantly, alive. He had war wounds, but he had survived. *Thank you, God. Thank you for sparing Ugo.*

When he hugged her to say hello, she felt her body melt into his.

"How are you?" he said. His Russian accent still reminded her of her papa and touched a nerve inside of her. She held him a little longer than just a quick hello.

"I'm fine. I heard you were in the Pacific," she stammered.

He nodded. "Yes, that's where I got the scar and the injury to my leg."

"It must be difficult to move the furniture with your injury."

He smiled. "I don't move furniture anymore. I bought the business. Other people do the moving. I keep the books."

"Oh, Ugo, that's wonderful."

"Yes, it is wonderful. I worked hard. I saved money. I found the American dream." He smiled wistfully. "It's cold out here. Why don't we go somewhere and have a hot cocoa?"

She laughed a short, nervous laugh. "Yes, let's do that. I could use something warm to drink."

They walked silently. The only sound was the snow crunching under their feet. They were both lost in their own thoughts. Thoughts of the past. Thoughts of each other.

Alina couldn't believe how affected she was by seeing Ugo. She knew she'd missed him, but until she saw him again, alive, in the flesh, she hadn't realized how much. He was a trusted friend who'd been with her through some very difficult times, and now, when she looked at him, she remembered those times. If it hadn't been for Ugo's tender prompting when she'd seen him on the street all those years ago, she would never have taken a class and learned English. They'd walked to English class together, two foreigners lost in an overwhelming country trying to find their way. But no matter how hard things were for him, he was always willing to listen to her problems and offer help or advice. She glanced up at him and was deeply touched by the memories of his warmth and caring.

"It's really quite chilly," he said, pulling his muffler tighter. "Not freezing like Russia, but for New York, it's cold."

"It is." She didn't know what else to say to him. And in a way, she was afraid to sit across from him at a table where he could see her eyes and all the feelings they would reveal. What if he'd found someone, even married? She felt she should ask before they got to the restaurant so he wouldn't see the raw emotion on her face if he told her there was a woman in his life. After all, she should expect that he was with someone. She had pushed him away. What was he to do, spend his life alone? If he said he had a wife, she would have to accept it.

"Ugo?"

"Yes?"

They were a few feet from the restaurant. How could she ask? She couldn't.

He opened the door for her. *Always the gentleman.*

After they were shown to a quiet corner table, he helped her with her coat and the chair. The room was dimly lit. He removed his coat and sat down across from her. There he was, just inches away from her. His eyes locked with hers. Alina didn't want to ask, but she had to know the answer to her most vital question.

"How have you been?" he asked. "You look beautiful."

"I've been alright, but a lot of things have happened since I last saw you," Alina said. "The house burnt down,"

"When?"

"Last month. A fire started in the middle of the night."

"Joey?"

"He's alright. Thank God. Klara is alright, too."

"Where are you living?"

"Well, Trevor, my husband, was robbed and murdered."

"Murdered? My God!"

"Yes. The police said he was on his way home when he was robbed and shot. They said he had been out playing cards. I suppose he was probably carrying a lot of cash. I don't know how a thief would have known that, but he always wore very expensive clothes and a lot of jewelry."

"New York can be a dangerous place," Ugo said, shaking his head.

"That's true. I feel bad about Trevor being killed. But I have to tell you the truth. I am relieved, too."

"He was abusing you, wasn't he?"

She nodded.

"I knew it. I wanted to kill him myself. Sometimes."

"You?"

"No, I didn't do it, Alina. I would never kill a man."

"I didn't think so," she said.

"Even a man who deserved it, like Trevor. You know, I'd see you with a black eye, and I wanted to beat the hell out of him. But I knew that you wanted me to stay out of it."

"Yes, I did. And I'm glad that you took my feelings into consideration."

"I don't know if I should ask this, but do you need some money. I mean, with the house gone, I can give you some money to help you out for a while."

"I have plenty. Trevor and I were never legally divorced. I inherited everything."

"Oh." He cleared his throat. "So, I suppose you plan to reopen another house?"

"No, I don't, actually. He left me well provided for. I don't need the money. So, I am not going to open another brothel."

She saw the relief in his eyes. Alina wanted to ask him if he was married. It was on the tip of her tongue, but she couldn't say the words.

"And you, how are you?" she said instead.

"I survived the Japanese." He smiled. "Like I said, I have my own business now. So, I suppose I am doing fine."

"You suppose?"

He looked directly into her eyes. "I don't have you."

She almost choked on her water. "Are you married?" There it was. It came out when she least expected to ask it….

"I never wanted anyone else after I met you, Alina. No, I am not married."

Can we start over? She wanted to ask him, but it was so hard to ask.

"I loved you, Alina. I still love you."

Her eyes welled up with tears. "Ugo, I don't have the house anymore. I won't be involved with that sort of thing anymore because I don't have to. I don't know how to say this…"

"Just say it, Alina." His eyes were glassy with tears, too.

"I'd like to try again."

"Alina, really? I can't believe it. I've been in love with you all this time, but I was such a stubborn, stupid man. So many times, I wanted to go and beg you to be mine no matter what you were doing with the house. But I didn't. I couldn't. I let pride get in the way of happiness. But right now, as I sit here looking into your eyes, I am grateful to God for bringing you back to me. I will be good to you, Alina. I will be good to you for the rest of my days on this earth."

He reached across the table and took her hand in his. A spark ran through her as he gently squeezed her hand. How could such a small gesture be more sensual than the lovemaking she'd shared with Johan and Trevor?

Alina took his hand and held it to her cheek. She longed for him to kiss her, but even though she'd been a madam of a brothel, she was still modest and shy, and she couldn't lean over and kiss him in public. *I am so many different women. I ran a whorehouse with perfect efficiency. A house where anything could happen and did happen. And yet, here I sit across the table from a man who has captured my heart, and I am once again like a child, a virgin, afraid and unsure.*

They sat in that café until the sun began to set, holding hands and sharing the feeling of the sweet tenderness of new love.

"I should go," Alina said. "It's getting dark. I should go and prepare dinner for Joey."

Ugo nodded.

"Has Joey been home alone all day?"

"No."

"Can I walk you home?"

Alina cleared her throat. It was time she told him. "Klara is staying with me until she buys a house. She's watching Joey. We are friends."

"My ex-wife is living with you?"

Alina nodded and looked away, afraid she and Ugo would be torn apart again.

"After the fire, she had no place to go. She is a good friend to me, Ugo."

There was silence. Alina was afraid that Ugo would walk away from her. But instead, he started laughing. "My ex-wife and my true love are best friends. Well, it's better than if the two of you were enemies, right?"

"Yes, it is. And she is a good person. You two were just not right for each other."

"I know that. She and I are like fire and ice. We fought like there was no tomorrow. But, for the sake of our relationship and your friendship, I am going to try to get along with Klara."

"She will be moving out on her own soon. But she and I will always be friends. And I should tell you now because it is only fair that you know. Klara is opening a brothel of her own. I will have nothing to do with it." Alina waited for his answer, nervous.

"You've decided not to be involved?" he asked.

"No. I am done with that life. I am going to give her the money to open it. But I will not be a part of the business. I did it because I needed the security. Now I have plenty. I don't need to do that anymore."

"Well, what can I say? I wish Klara a lot of luck in her new business." He smiled. "You know, I want to tell you something."

"Sure, go on."

"When I bought the moving company, my first thought, my very first thought, was, maybe, just maybe now, Alina will sell that house and marry me. I wanted that more than anything. I thought about it every night, even when I was in Okinawa."

Alina cocked her head to one side. "Ugo?"

"Yes."

"I have a question, and you must tell me the truth." She looked into his eyes. "Did you burn down my house?"

"Alina! No, I did not! How could you think that?"

"I didn't until now. It just came to me."

"No, Alina. I would never have done that. I wanted you to come to me of your own free will, not because you lost your business. Do you believe me?"

"Yes, I believe you."

"I would never do that to you. No matter how much I wanted you, I could never hurt you."

"I'm sorry. I had to ask. I had to know."

"I understand."

"Forgive me for doubting you?"

"Yes, but I wish you knew that you could trust me. You've always been so afraid to trust. I never have and will never betray you, Alina."

It was not like her to be openly affectionate in public. Still, she wanted to let Ugo know she believed him, so she leaned across the table and kissed him gently.

Then he helped Alina with her coat, and they walked towards her home.

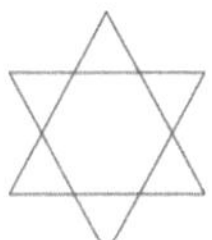

thirty-five

Alina

January 1946

UGO AND ALINA did not tell anyone about their decision to become a couple for almost a month. Alina was not looking forward to Ugo and Klara spending time together. She knew they were a volatile mix, so she tried to keep them apart as long as possible.

Ugo and Alina met secretly at cafés where they sipped coffee or tea and held hands. Their relationship had the innocent ideals of youth. When they were together, Ugo and Alina were like teenagers tasting life for the first time. They took long walks in the evening and made wishes on stars. They laughed easily and shared kisses in the rain. It was as if all that they had suffered in their pasts now lay buried deep beneath a blanket of love that sheltered them.

One cold January afternoon, when the sun's rays looked like tiny diamonds on the freshly fallen snow, Alina sat across from Ugo in a busy restaurant. They were enjoying a light lunch. "Klara knows you are seeing me?" Ugo asked.

"Not yet."

"You think she'll be upset?"

"I don't think so. In fact, she's always told me that you and I should be together."

"Really?"

"Yes. She is a wonderful friend to me, Ugo. But I know you and Klara have had your differences. And I know you two can't be in the same room for five minutes without a fight."

"Yes, we did. That's for sure. But we were so young when we got married. Then she was here in America without me for a long time. While I was still in Russia, trying to find a way to earn enough money to come here, she was watching people here live a life she could only dream of. Then, when I finally came here, I couldn't provide for her properly." He hesitated. "At the time, I hoped she would come back to me. But once we lost our daughter, it all ended for us. It was just not meant to be."

"Does that make you sad?"

"It did make me sad, not so much over losing Klara. What brought me to my knees was the death of my little girl. I didn't think I could ever get over it." He took her hand. "But, then, Alina, there was you. You didn't know it, but you were the only flicker of light in my dark life for a long time." Then he added, "I'll always miss my child. But now that you and I are together, I know what real love is. And I understand why Klara and I were not destined to be together. You bring me joy, Alina. I am far too happy to hold any grudges. I think Klara and I can be friends now. At least from my standpoint. I would like to see her."

"You make me very happy too. And I, too, have to admit that I was stubborn about not giving up the brothel. I was so afraid not to have my own money."

"Well, now we both have plenty of money. But you want to know something funny?"

"Of course."

"You promise not to be angry."

"I promise."

"In a way, I wish you didn't inherit all that money from Trevor. I wish I had been the one to provide for you. As I told you, I bought the business to earn enough money to make you feel secure. I wanted to be able to do that for you. I wanted to be your husband, your provider. I wanted to be the man who took good care of you. Ach … I am really from the old country. I still have old country ideas, I suppose."

"We wasted so much time," she said.

"Yes, we did. But then, by some miracle, you were on the street. Our eyes met. I had to say hello. It was as if the stars aligned for us…"

"I never knew you were so poetic." She smiled.

"I mean it. It was very magical for me. Then when you agreed to go to the café with me, I couldn't believe it. I was afraid that my heart was singing so loud that you might be able to hear it."

"You really are poetic today." She giggled.

"Alina." He took both of her hands in his. "I want to ask you something."

"Sure, what is it?"

"Alina, will you marry me?"

Her face shone with love and joy. "Yes," she whispered. Tears began to swell in her eyes.

"You will," he said, his voice choked up as a tear dropped down his cheek. Then he lifted both of her hands to his lips.

"I will." She giggled.

He got up from his chair. Then he pulled Alina to her feet, took her into his arms, and kissed her.

"Ugo, not here. Everyone is looking."

He smiled. "Let's hurry up and get married. Maybe we can finally be alone, and I can get a decent kiss." He laughed. She laughed, too.

thirty-six

Alina

IN EARLY FEBRUARY 1946, Alina and Ugo Blok were married in a small civil ceremony conducted by the justice of the peace. Ugo's ex-wife, Klara, was present, as was Joey, Alina's son. Ugo looked handsome in a dark, well-made suit and red tie. Alina wore a dove gray dress made of cashmere. Despite neither of them being a virgin, they both decided to wait until their wedding night to make love for the first time.

After the bride and groom were pronounced man and wife, everyone in the bridal party went to a nearby restaurant for dinner. In a few months, Alina would be twenty-five, and this was already her third marriage. The first, to Johan, was not legal because of the Nuremberg laws.

However, it had always felt like a real marriage to Alina. Johan was tender and kind, but she had been too young and unprepared. The second, to Trevor, had been forced, a marriage born out of fear and desperation.

But the third, this marriage to Ugo, was a union of love. As they held hands together, Alina felt, for the first time in her life, that she might have a chance at true happiness. After today, she would never again face the world alone.

For a moment, she thought of her parents, Gilde, Lotti, and Lev. The only thing that could have made this day brighter would have been their presence. If her family had met Ugo, she knew they would have come to love him the way she did. He was so good to her. She smiled wryly. They probably would have wanted her to get married under a canopy. She wouldn't have minded. And she doubted that Ugo would have cared. A canopy. A beautiful canopy, a chuppah.

Well, if it was not meant to be that she married under a canopy, at least she had finally found love, which was the most important thing in life. When Ugo had asked Alina to marry him, she'd gone home that same day and tried to call Lotti. Alina dialed the operator and gave her the number she had for Lotti in Berlin. The operator tried to place the call, but the call would not go through. And, thus far, Lotti had not answered Alina's letter.

Well, if I have lost everyone, at least I have my husband, son, and best friend for life in Klara. I am truly blessed. Alina squeezed Ugo's hand as she thought.

Klara was striking with her red hair, high black heels, and green satin dress. She and Ugo had finally made peace after their tumultuous marriage. It was easier than Ugo thought it would be. In fact, Klara was kind and acted more like a sister to him than an ex-wife. Ugo had forgotten how devastatingly beautiful Klara was until she saw her dressed to the nines that night.

But Ugo only had eyes for Alina. From the first time he saw her on the boat with Johan, he knew she was different from any other woman he'd ever known. She was headstrong and smart like Klara. But unlike Klara, Alina was sincere and devoted. Every instinct reassured him that she would not be looking for another man, a richer man, a better man. She was his, and he was hers. This was a true marriage in the eyes of God.

That night, when Alina and Ugo were alone, she was struck with a sudden overwhelming affection when she saw how nervous he was. She wanted to protect him, mother him, and let him know that everything would be all right from then on, no matter what she had to do. His hands trembled as he took her into his arms, and for a long time, he just held her. Then his lips met hers, and she felt his face wet with tears.

The only other time she'd ever seen him weak or vulnerable in all the years she'd known him was when his daughter died. Otherwise, no matter what trials and tribulations life flung his way, he faced them like a lion. But not tonight. Tonight, Ugo was a lamb in her arms. The strongest man she'd ever known, weak now because of his love for her. Like the tale of Samson and Delilah, she would never betray him the way Delilah betrayed Samson. Alina could see in Ugo's eyes that he was humbled by his love for her. Yes, this certainly was a new side of her husband; he was as tender as a new blade of grass. He was shy, like a boy. He was a man surrendered to love.

She watched him as he undressed her.

"I never thought, never believed in my wildest dreams, that this would happen. I forced thoughts of you out of my mind because it hurt too much to think of you," Ugo said, his voice soft but choked up, and then he kissed her before she could answer.

He made love to her even more lovingly than Johan and with far more passion than she'd felt from any man in her life.

"I will worship you for the rest of my days on earth," he whispered in her ear as they became one. And she held tight to him, surrendering her need to be strong, her need for control. If only for a short while in his arms, Alina would yield and finally allow her love for him to conquer her fear of trust. She'd carried the weight of the world on her shoulders since Johan died. It felt good to let her guard down and finally trust another person, knowing that Ugo would not let her fall.

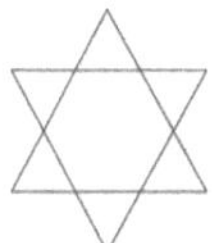

thirty-seven
Lotti

Berlin
February 1946

ONE EVENING, Lotti returned to her apartment to find Berni had gone. All her things were gone, and she left no forwarding note or address.

Berni had given no indication that she planned to leave, and Lotti had no idea where to begin to look for her. She knew that Berni was damaged. Her heart and soul were tainted with pain, which made her introverted and afraid. Lotti had often tried to help Berni, but Berni was too resistant.

Nothing ever came of Lotti's attempt to make a match between Berni and Gabe. Neither of them had any interest in the other. But Lotti and Gabe became friends, and on occasion, out of loneliness, they were lovers. Lotti didn't delude herself into believing that a man more than ten years her junior would not tire of her when he returned home to the United States. But for now, he was someone to fill the hours. She was not in love with him. He was a good friend, nothing more.

Lotti didn't search for Berni. She was hurt that Berni disappeared without a word, but Lotti decided that if Berni wanted to go, she would not try to stop her. However, she wondered if Berni and Gabe might have slept together sometimes. Perhaps that was what drove Berni to leave. Berni might have felt like she was betraying Lotti.

Although in the beginning, when Lotti and Gabe first met, Lotti hoped to see Berni and Gabe as a couple. But once Lotti slept with Gabe, even though she knew there was no future, she wasn't sure she would have accepted Berni and Gabe as lovers if it had happened.

Maybe Berni sensed that and felt it best that she leave. Lotti couldn't be sure what had happened, but she thought this might have been the motive for Berni's disappearance. After Berni was gone, Lotti returned to the empty nights of quiet dinners alone. Although Berni hadn't been much company, at least she was there. Now, Lotti came home to an empty apartment again.

Lotti still had her job and continued volunteering at the DP camp. Sometimes, however, the work with displaced persons did not make her feel useful. It actually made her feel worse.

She'd taken the job hoping that by helping others, she might find peace, but what she found was that, in most cases, there was nothing she could do to ease the pain of the survivors. Then, something terrible happened.

She, Lotti, the girl who never held a grudge, never hated or condemned, realized that she'd grown into a bitter woman obsessed with hatred for the Nazi regime. Lotti found herself thinking about all she'd lost, and hatred grew inside of her like a cancer. She dreamed of murdering Nazi officers and awoke in a cold sweat.

Damn them, they'd stolen the lives of so many people, her included. She was aging rapidly for her years. Her anger and resentment were eating her from the inside out. Lotti knew she spent too much time alone in that apartment, consumed by rage. So, on rare nights, Gabe had time to see her, and she was glad for the company. And since he was an American GI, he had access to extra food, which he was generous enough to bring as a gift to her when he visited.

Gabe brought things that had become rare treasures because of their scarcity, a piece or two of fresh fruit, sometimes a can of sardines. And she had to admit, Gabe was a lot of fun, generous, very American. When he came to see her, she was able to forget herself and laugh for a few hours. He was handy and more than willing to help with repairs in her apartment. She appreciated all he did. But Lotti knew he was too young for her. His life was ahead of him. And even though she was only thirty-eight years old, she felt her life was over.

Oh, Lev, she thought. The years she'd spent with Lev were the golden years of her life. For a brief moment, she'd reached out and touched heaven; her soul had been joined with his, and she'd known pure joy. Yes, that was when she was truly living.

Now, Lotti merely existed. Getting up every morning, she followed the same routine. She washed her face, combed her hair, and looked in the mirror at the woman with sunken eyes who had once been such a carefree and blissful soul. Once, and it seemed like so long ago, these very same rooms where she now lived alone had been filled with love and laughter.

Her memories drifted back to her dear friends, the Margolis family. They would come to visit, and when their two daughters were young, the children ran through the rooms playing hide and seek and giggling. Michal had begged her children to sit down and behave, but Lotti never minded. She couldn't have children, and Gilde and Alina were like her own.

As the girls grew up, she'd bonded deeply with Alina, who was such a quiet girl. Lotti knew Alina had opened up to her in a way she never could to her mother. Lotti was glad to be there for Alina. And then Alina and Lotti's brother, Johan, had fallen in love and disappeared. Where were they now? "Alive, dead?" She spoke the words aloud, but there was no answer, only the echo of her own voice in the empty apartment. And little Gilde? Such a sweet and happy child she had been. What happened to Gilde? She'd boarded a train one day and rode out of their lives.

Lotti had never heard from her again. And poor Michal. What happened to her dear friend Michal, who never returned when she went to the police station to look for her husband? What had become of her? Or Taavi?

The last she'd seen of her husband's best friend and business part-ner, he was on the run like a hunted animal. Such a good man Taavi was, such a good friend to her and Lev. Yes, those days before the Nazis, those were the golden days, the days of pure delight. All that she had now were memories, memories of laughter, memories of love.

Some nights, she awoke crying from heartbreaking dreams of Lev. Dreams so real she could touch him, hear him. The yearning for the dreams to be reality was devastating. Dear tender Lev, his arms around her, the comfort of the warmth of his smile. Dreams from which she must awaken. *God, please,* she would think, *let me go on sleeping and living in this dream forever.* But she would always open her eyes to find she was still alone. Once upon a time, Lotti had lived a fairy tale. But today, this was all that was left of her life.

On a cold Wednesday morning, she got up and realized she had no food in the apartment. She had to go out to the market. It didn't really matter. She didn't feel like eating breakfast that morning. Many days, she had no appetite. Lotti had grown very thin and pale. She was off work today and wasn't volunteering at the DP camp. It was a good day to spend her time cleaning the apartment. Gabe said he was going to try to drop by on her day off, and he usually kept his promise. Lotti took the broom and began sweeping the kitchen when the downstairs doorbell rang. She smiled. Of course, it was Gabe.

Gabe walked three floors up and entered the apartment with a cloth sack and a letter.

"I brought some strudel and real coffee." He smiled.

"You're so good to me." Lotti smiled back and began boiling water for the coffee.

"This was in your mailbox." Gabe handed her a letter with strange postage. "I hope you don't mind that I brought it up. It looks like it's from America. You don't know anyone in America, do you?"

"No, no one in America." Lotti took the envelope, puzzled. But then her hands began to tremble when she recognized the hand-writing.

thirty-eight
Gilde

London
March 1946

GILDE'S CLASS was doing a recital that afternoon. She had a lot of work to do to put things together. The parents of the students had rented a hall. It wasn't really a hall. It was an empty apartment above a bakery. They'd only rented it for the day, but it was enough to have all the students very excited.

It wasn't extremely large. There was room for several chairs and a make-do stage that one of the student's fathers had built out of wood. Off the main room lay a small, ill-equipped kitchen where the girls would change their costumes.

It was a makeshift theater. However, it gave the students a thrill of excitement to be performing before an audience, even if the audience was only a group of parents, siblings, and family friends.

For Gilde, giving singing, dancing, and acting lessons to a group of children couldn't compare to the heady excitement of the applause of a crowd. But her depression from losing Alden took the fire out of that thrill for her. What once had been a childhood dream now paled in comparison to a happy home.

Her little school was not earning enough money to employ a nanny, so she had to care for Vicky herself. Although it was more difficult, she could no longer take long afternoon naps. At the same time, it was satisfying. Gilde bonded with her daughter in ways she could not when she was distracted by her stage career. The students took turns watching Vicky to enable Gilde to conduct the class. They usually took Vicky to her room when they finished rehearsing their particular segment of the recital.

The girls were all young; none seemed to mind helping Gilde, and for that, Gilde was grateful. Without their cooperation, she could never have kept the school open. Gilde still had occasional contact with the theatrical agent who'd represented her, and every so often, she was offered an audition. Twice, she had been selected for callbacks for a second audition, but she'd never been cast for the part.

Although she would never admit it to anyone, sometimes she put Vicky in her buggy and walked by the hospital, hoping to get a glimpse of Alden. Of course, she never did. She often wondered how he was and if Jane had given birth to the baby yet. The thought of him with Jane, holding Jane, kissing her, was painful, but she thought about it often. There was no stopping her mind. Visions of Alden and Jane played like a film clip on a circular reel, going over and over on a movie screen inside her head.

Vicky was growing quickly, and she had begun attempting to walk. She was stubborn and difficult, crying when she fell or didn't get her way. The students in Gilde's class were finding it difficult to control the toddler. Now that there was going to be a recital, Gilde was forced to hire a babysitter. She found a teenage girl who was willing to watch Vicky during the show, so Gilde was free to help her students with costume changes and prompts. Gilde brought several of Vicky's toys and put them in the corner of the makeshift dressing room.

The babysitter was trying to entertain Vicky, who was fussy and wanted to explore the contents of the kitchen cabinets. Vicky was full of energy; even for her teenage sitter, she was a handful. At three that afternoon, the parents began arriving and getting seated. There was chaos and an air of giddy excitement in the dressing room. The students were nervous.

They each wanted to be the star of the show, at least in their own adoring parents' eyes. And Gilde wanted them to enjoy their little theater class. After all, their parents made it possible for her to keep her apartment and raise her daughter.

Most of her students were wealthy girls with indulging parents who didn't mind paying a nice sum for lessons, especially from an actress on the stage in some of London's finest theaters. All of them were rich girls except one of the students. She was a girl who had come as a guest with a wealthy friend. The girl was a shy, introverted youngster who had captured Gilde's heart instantly, so Gilde extended an invitation for the girl to attend the school without charge.

Her name was Kassandra, but the others called her Cassy. And once she got on stage, Cassy was like a different person. She emerged from her cocoon like a butterfly, and it was obvious that she was more gifted than the rest. But, regardless of their talent, Gilde loved all of her students.

The production consisted of small skits from American musicals that the students had selected themselves, and Gilde had approved. Only three boys were in the class, so some of the females also performed male parts. The small kitchen was crowded with people. Two girls were practicing their song from the Gershwin musical called *Crazy Girl*, and they came over and asked Gilde to watch. "Please, Mrs. Thornbury, can we do our skit for you one more time before we go on stage. We'll do it quietly so that no one will hear out in the audience?"

"Yes, of course," Gilde said.

The two students stood opposite each other, singing.

"You're a little off-key. Try again," Gilde said, sitting on a kitchen stool and giving them directions.

The girls sang together much more beautifully this time. "That was perfect!" Gilde said. A case of pre-stage fright, Gilde thought to herself and smiled.

"Is my lipstick on all right?" another of the girls asked Gilde.

"My goodness, it's a bit smeared. Here, let me help you," Gilde said, taking a rag and wiping the girl's lips.

"Mrs. Thornbury!" Cassy screamed. "Mrs. Thornbury, come quick."

Gilde jumped up as the chair moved from under her and slid across the wood floor. Then Gilde ran towards the sound of Cassy's voice. Cassy stood in the doorway.

"What is it? What happened?" Gilde heard Vicky wailing and didn't wait for an answer but followed the sound of Vicky's voice to the hallway outside the apartment. There, she found Vicky lying at the bottom of the stairs.

"Oh my God," Gilde said, rushing down the wooden stairs, her feet barely touching the ground.

"I don't know how this happened. I don't know how Vicky got out of the apartment and fell down the stairs. I'm sorry, Mrs. Thornbury, I am. But I was watching her, and then I got distracted by all the singing and dancing, and I am so sorry, but she wandered off..."

"Call for a taxi," she yelled to the two girls, who stood frozen with fear at the top of the stairs. "Hurry."

Vicky's face was covered in blood, and she couldn't get up. "It's all right, my darling, it's all right," Gilde whispered into her daughter's ear, even though she wasn't sure she believed her own words. *At least she's crying. I know she's alive.*

"Never mind about the taxi. I have a motorcar." One of the fathers came racing downstairs. "Let me get it, and I'll meet you in front of the building. We'll take her straight to the hospital."

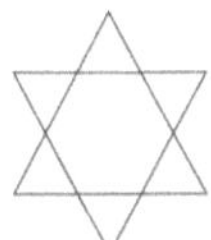

thirty-nine

Lotti

Berlin
March 1946

A LETTER FROM AMERICA? Who would send her a letter from America? The handwriting. Could it be? Was it really possible? Was this a miracle from God? Lotti ripped the envelope open with trembling hands. She read the signature before she began the letter. As soon as she read the words, she knew she was right; it was Alina, and it was a miracle from God. "With love, your friend, your sister, always, Alina." The tears began to stream down Lotti's face.

"What is it?" Gabe asked.

"It's a letter from Alina. Do you remember me telling you about Alina?"

He nodded.

She read the letter in silence, and for several minutes, neither of them spoke. "My God, Gabe, Alina is alive. She's alive."

forty

Gilde

London
March 1946

EVERYTHING from when Gilde found Vicky at the bottom of the stairs was a blur. The ride to the hospital. The nurses and doctors put Vicky on a stretcher. The medical personnel tried to shuffle her out of the examining room, but she refused.

"Her nose is broken. And her leg is broken. But she should be all right," the doctor said.

"Oh my God," Gilde said. "Oh my God." Her hand flew up to her throat. "Is Alden Thornbury working tonight? Is he here now? Please, I have to see him." Gilde was almost hysterical. She wanted Alden. He was the only doctor she trusted with her daughter.

"He was here all day. He left about an hour or so ago. We can help you. There are plenty of good doctors here to help you." A nurse with a starched white uniform put her arm on Gilde's shoulder, trying to be the voice of reason.

"No, I am his ex-wife. This is his daughter. I know he would want to be here. Please call him."

forty-one
Alden

IT HAD BEEN another long and grueling day at the hospital. Even though the war was over, there were still so many people needing medical care all the time.

It wasn't as bad as it was during the bombings, but being a doctor was and always would be an all-consuming job. When people were ill, they looked to him for relief. They looked up from their hospital beds with eyes glassed over in misery.

Alden wished he was supernatural and could heal the sick with just a touch. Sometimes, when overwhelmed, he thought about how Jesus must have felt when crowds begged him to heal them. But he wasn't Jesus. He knew he wasn't a god. So many of the other doctors thought they were. Alden knew he was just a man with some medical skills that he hoped to use in order to do good in the world.

Alden thought about his day and all the people he'd treated. He hoped they would make it through the night. *I can't be there for twenty-four hours a day. I am only human.* His stomach growled as he realized it had been seven hours since he'd last eaten. There was nothing to eat in the pantry.

Since Jane left, he'd been eating his meals at the hospital cafeteria or not at all. It seemed to be impossible to find the time to go shopping for food. He was either exhausted or working. He found a box of crackers on the shelf. Taking it down, he opened it to find three old, moldy, broken pieces. He had to laugh. Even he wouldn't eat that.

And after the terrible food he'd eaten at the hospital, something had to be totally inedible for him to turn it away. He was too tired to go to a restaurant, so he'd have to wait until morning. Leaning down, he took off his shoes and sank into the sofa. Then he rubbed one of his feet. It was swollen. That was to be expected. His shoulders ached, too. Very strange, but the only thing he missed about Jane after leaving him was the back rubs she gave him when he got home. But when she miscarried the baby, it traumatized her, and she changed.

She was sure it was because their marriage had been cursed. "It's because I stole you from Gilde. God is angry with me, Alden. I can feel it, and I am scared. I must leave you, or something even worse will happen. I just know it. Our marriage is built on adultery, and losing this baby is proof that we are being punished."

Alden didn't believe in a vengeful God. But from the day she lost the baby, Jane began to descend into a web of fear and madness. Finally, he decided that she was right and that it would probably be best if they said goodbye.

She blamed God's wrath for even the smallest thing that went wrong. She was distant from him and could not make love with him because she was afraid that if she could get pregnant again, she would surely prompt God's rage. And, if he were completely truthful with himself, Alden knew he was never in love with Jane. He was sorry they'd lost the baby, but maybe it was for the best. The marriage was a farce.

Every time they made love, he thought about Gilde. That was not fair to Jane, and he knew it. Jane deserved better. And, somehow, Alden believed that maybe God had Jane's best interest at heart when she miscarried. Now she was free to find someone who really loved her like he should have. And Alden? He was alone, but he was free to marry his work, his second true love after Gilde. Devotion to his job as a healer became his top priority in life. The phone rang just as he was about to massage his other foot.

Another emergency at the hospital? He got up to answer.

forty-two

Gilde

ALDEN RAN INTO THE HOSPITAL. His hair was askew, his face pale and tired, but when they called and said Gilde needed him, he didn't hesitate.

"Alden, it's Vicky." Gilde grabbed Alden's sleeve as he approached the emergency treatment room, where a group of doctors and nurses surrounded Gilde's daughter.

"I know. They called me from the desk and told me everything. Let me get in and see her."

Gilde started to follow after him, but Alden stopped her. "It's easier to work on a child when the mother is not in the room. Please, Gilde. Wait outside," he said. His voice was soft and kind. She wanted to cry.

Gilde moved out of the way and watched from the door as Alden's gentle, capable hands worked magic on her child, the little girl they both loved. God, how Gilde missed him. She dared not think about how much she still loved him.

Instead, she wondered if Jane had had the baby yet or when she was due. He had another life now, another child. But seeing him there treating Vicky filled her heart with longing for him and their past together. He moved to the other side of the bed to adjust a machine. It was hard for her to watch him caring for Vicky. The way he was with the child brought so many memories flooding back to her.

After all, Alden had been Vicky's father, if not biological, still the only father she'd ever known. He'd changed her diapers and walked the floor with her when she was teething. *Oh God, Alden, I miss you.* Then, a painful thought came to her. Did Alden ever think of Vicky now that he had or would soon have his biological child?

It was nearly midnight when Vicky's treatment was done, and she rested comfortably. Alden stood at the sink, washing his hands. Then he walked out of the room and found Gilde still standing in the doorway where he'd left her over four hours ago.

"You should have sat down and waited in the waiting room. You've been standing here a long time."

"I couldn't leave, Alden. Is Vicky going to be all right?"

"She's banged up, that's for sure. But, she'll be all right," Alden said, gently patting Gilde's shoulder.

"This should never have happened," Gilde said. "I don't know how to be a mother or even a good person for that matter. I am neglectful. I just can't seem to do the right thing. Not with anything in my life." The exhaustion and stress of the day brought tears to her eyes. She wiped them with the back of her hand before they fell onto her cheeks.

"Come on, let me buy you a cup of tea," Alden said. "You look like you could use it."

"How about something stronger? Like a gin and tonic?"

"Sorry, no, there's no alcohol in the hospital cafeteria. Although, I've often thought that there should be. Patients' families could use it sometimes," he said, smiling.

"I know, it was just wishful thinking," Gilde said, glancing into the room where Vicky was asleep. "Are you sure it's all right if we leave her?"

"Yes, it's fine. The nurses will tend to her. And, I gave her some powerful painkillers so she should sleep through the night." He smiled. "So, since we can't get that gin and tonic here, let's go and have some tea."

"Tea it is," she said, sighing.

He got two cups of steaming tea brewed several hours ago that were a little stale, but they both added milk and sugar. Then, they sat down at a table in the corner. Only three other people were in the room, and they were all sitting separately. Two of them were women, probably wives or mothers of patients. The other was an old man. The cafeteria was eerily quiet.

"I'm sorry to have had them call you. I knew you were just getting home from work. It was selfish of me. But you're the only person I feel comfortable with to take care of Vicky."

"I'm glad you called me."

"I feel so guilty," Gilde said. "this should never have happened. I am a terrible mother, Alden." Then she hesitated and looked away. "And I was a terrible wife, too."

"No, Gilde. You weren't a terrible wife, and you aren't a terrible mother. You just have a talent that drives you to pursue it. You can't help it."

"You mean the theater?" she asked.

"Of course. I know how much you love being on stage. You shine when you're up there, bright as the sun. I just couldn't take that away from you. I loved you too much, Gilde."

She shook her head and picked up the spoon to stir her tea. It felt like she should do something with her hands. "I'm not working as an actress. I haven't been on a show since you left, and I don't intend to do another one. I've auditioned a few times, but my heart wasn't in it anymore. I guess it showed because I didn't get any of the parts I tried out for," she whispered.

"But why?"

She shrugged. "After you left, the applause, the audience, none of it mattered. I no longer had the same feeling when I went on stage. You see, it was you, Alden, you were my greatest fan. You were the fire that kept me going. I just couldn't be the entertainer I was before. It just wasn't in me anymore. I guess I realized that I lost the best thing that ever happened to me when I lost you." Tears had formed in the corners of her eyes and threatened to spill down her cheeks. She wiped them hard with her hand. "I'm sorry, Alden. We shouldn't even be talking about this. You and Jane…"

"Jane and I are separated. We're getting a divorce."

"What? Why? What about the baby?" she asked, looking deeply into his eyes. She felt a myriad of emotions. She was happy and sad at the same time. He looked older, more weathered. But he was here, sitting across from her, and she longed to reach out and touch his hand. She didn't want him to suffer, but her heart sang at the news of his freedom, hoping they could be together again.

"She lost the baby. She's very superstitious, and she was sure that our marriage was cursed."

"Oh…" Gilde said. "Oh, Alden." She cleared her throat, suddenly feeling ashamed of her happiness. It was a horrible thing to lose a child. And once she had loved Jane as a sister. Those feelings were not gone, not really. Gilde was confused, happy, sad, guilty, shameful, and in love. "I should say I am sorry. But the truth is I am not. I mean, I am sorry that she miscarried, but I am not sorry that you are separated. Oh God, I am a terrible person."

"You missed me that much?"

"More than you could ever know."

"I missed you every day, Gilde. I missed Vicky, too. All I ever really wanted was for you to be happy."

"And once you left, I realized that all I ever needed to be happy was you. Oh, Alden, I am selfish and vain and have more faults than I can count. But I love you. I love Vicky, and by God, I really love you."

"Gilde." He took her hand in his. "Do you want to get back together? Give it another try?"

"More than I can say."

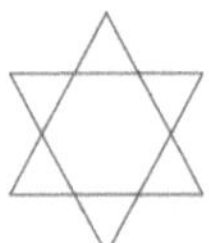

forty-three

Alina

Atlantic Ocean
April 1946

ALINA WAS quiet during most of the voyage on the ship from New York back to Germany. As Joey slept, Alina and Ugo walked on the deck one night.

"The accommodations are much nicer this time than they were when we came to America. Remember? When I was with Johan, you were on your way to the new land from Russia."

"How could I ever forget? That voyage changed my life. And can you believe that we are in first class now? We were in third class then."

She looked around at the first-class accommodations and shook her head in amazement. She clasped her throat with her hand as she looked at Ugo. When they first came to America, they ate at long wooden tables. Now, they took their meals in a lovely dining room with crisp white tablecloths. Before, they slept on cots as hard as a concrete floor. Now, they slept in a comfortable bed in a private stateroom.

"I remember. I remember all of it. The smell, too," he said. "Ach, those terrible smells." He put his arm around her.

"I don't mean this to make you jealous, but I couldn't help but think of Johan when we set sail. He and I boarded a boat just like this one with such hopes and dreams. And he died so young."

"You loved him?"

"Yes, but not the way I love you."

"Is that good?"

"It is. I truly love you, Ugo. I'm just feeling a little nostalgic. Do you remember the first time you and I met? It was on that ship. You helped me try to heal Johan's infected wound. Do you recall?"

"How could I ever forget? I thought you were so beautiful. But, of course, at the time, I never dreamed that you and I would be together. I was coming to America to be with my wife. And you were going to be married."

"It's interesting the way life works itself out," she said.

"It is." He caressed her gently. "Are you cold?"

"A little."

He took off his jacket and put it around her shoulders. "Excited to see Lotti?"

"Yes, and nervous too. I am going to have to tell her what happened to Johan. She will be heartbroken to learn that her brother is dead. Besides that, she is my only hope of ever finding my parents and sister. If she can't tell me anything about them, I have no other place to look. They will be lost to me forever."

"Well, we'll soon be there, and I'll be with you. At your side through all of it."

"My husband."

"Yes, forever, your husband, your ally, your best friend. And you, my darling Alina, you are my wife."

forty-four

Lotti and Alina

Berlin
April 1946

AS ALINA WALKED into the apartment building where she'd stayed with Lotti and Lev many years ago, chills ran through her entire body. When she was just a young girl, this neighborhood, her family, and her friends were all she knew of the world.

Memories, she was surrounded by memories. Walks to the subway station with Lotti in the morning as they went to work at the orphanage. The faint smell of perspiration mixed with packed lunches as everyone waited on the benches. The feeling of being suffocated as people were pressed together on the crowded train heading downtown.

And the holidays she shared with her parents, Gilde, Lotti, and Lev. The women would all gather at Lotti's apartment or Alina's home and start cooking and baking early in the morning. She could still smell the warm, homey yeast of the challah as it baked, filling the house with the fragrance of love and family. Before she could take the steps through the door of Lotti's apartment that would lead her back into the past, Alina stood trembling on the stoop for several minutes, unable to move.

My God, Berlin has changed. Alina was truly shaken by what she saw all around her. She'd come to Lotti's apartment as a child, and now it was the aftermath of a war zone. The bombings had all but destroyed the city. Alina found it hard to breathe as she looked at the broken buildings and the rubble in the streets. Hitler had not only murdered millions, but his sick dreams had also massacred the city of her birth. A city she loved.

"Knock, Mommy. Why aren't you knocking on the door?" Joey asked as he cocked his head. Alina turned to look at her son. How could she ever explain to him why she was hesitating?

"Give her a chance, Joe. Mom needs a minute," Ugo said, putting his arm around Joey's shoulder. Alina smiled at Ugo. He was so good to Joey, nothing like Trevor. She said a silent thanks to God for her husband and son. Then she gingerly knocked on the door that would open the Pandora's box to her history.

A woman wearing a dark forest green dress opened the door. It was Lotti. But it was a much older, more somber version of the light-hearted girl who Alina remembered.

"Alina…" Lotti said. Her voice was the same, and hearing it brought Alina to tears. Lotti grabbed Alina in her arms and hugged her hard. Then they were both crying.

"Lotti…" Alina looked into Lotti's face and wiped a tear off Lotti's cheek.

They stood like that in the doorway for several minutes until Lotti glanced up and saw the rest of Alina's family just standing there, looking out of place. "I'm sorry. Where are my manners? Please, come in. Come in, all of you."

Ugo helped Joey over the steps to enter the apartment. Alina followed.

"Sit, please. Let me get you a cup of tea. I bought cookies for you when you told me you were coming. Let me get them." Lotti was nervous and scattered. Her hands were trembling. She went to the kitchen and began filling cups with tea. She dropped a mug, and it broke.

Alina heard the glass break in the other room.

"Lotti, let me help you," Alina said as she entered the kitchen, leaving Ugo and Joey in the living room.

"You look beautiful, Alina. I … when I got your letter, I…" Lotti sunk into a kitchen chair and began to weep. Heartfelt sobs came from deep in her throat. "I thought you were dead. I feared you were dead…"

Alina knelt beside her old friend and hugged her.

"Johan? I assume the man and child in the living room are your husband and son. Do you know what happened to Johan?"

"Oh, Lotti, yes. I do."

"Tell me, please, tell me where is my brother…"

"He became ill. We were on our way to America. We couldn't get married in Germany. The Nuremberg laws… He thought it best we get out, and he was right. Oh, Lotti. I don't know how to tell you this. All I can say is I am sorry, Lotti. Johan died on the ship to America. Joey is his son."

"My brother is dead." Her face was pale. "Joey? The boy out there in the living room is Joey? He is my nephew?"

"I didn't introduce you. I'm sorry. I am afraid I'm a bit over-whelmed. It's all happening so fast. Yes, that is Joey, my son by Johan. Your nephew. And the man in your living room is Ugo, my husband. He is helping me to raise Joey. I hope you will be a little comforted knowing that Ugo is very good to Joey."

"Joey is sick?"

"He was very sick, yes. With polio when he was young," Alina said.

"Did Johan see his son before he died?"

"No." Alina shook her head. "He died on the boat before I had the chance to tell him I was pregnant. He never knew…"

"Oh, Alina. It must have been hard for you. So many people that we knew and loved are gone. Lev was murdered."

"By who? The Nazis?"

"Yes. My Lev. He's gone."

"Oh, my God, Lotti, I am so sorry."

"Yes, Lev was murdered."

"I'm so sorry," Alina whispered, shaking her head.

"Well, it's been years that he has been gone. I should be used to it." She forced a smile. "But I am not. The truth is, I think about Lev all the time. I don't suppose you ever get used to it. Not really."

"No, I don't believe you do," Alina said. "I still think of Johan."

"I'm glad you found someone who you love and who loves you, who is good to your son. I am glad you're not alone," Lotti said.

"Ugo is Russian like Lev and Papa," Alina said. "His accent was the first thing I noticed about him. Sometimes, I think it is what originally made me fall in love with him. It reminded me of my papa." She smiled through her tears.

"Russian," Lotti said, smiling, her face wet with tears as well.

"Have you heard anything from my parents or my sister? Do you know where I can find them?"

"No. I have heard nothing since your father was arrested and your mother left to find him. I've tried to write to Gilde, but she never answered. I stayed in this apartment because I have been hoping that all of you would return someday," Lotti said.

"This was the last address that all of us remembered. A few years ago, your father came to see me. The war was still raging through the city. Jews were being hunted like animals. It was a terrible time in Germany and any country that Hitler occupied. Somehow, your papa escaped from a concentration camp. I didn't know what to do. I hope I didn't make a mistake, but I sent him away. You see, I knew it wasn't safe for him here at my house. After all, my neighbors never trusted me. They were watching me. People were betraying each other left and right. It was hard to trust anyone. And, remember, I had been married to a Jew. Plenty of the neighbors made it clear to me that they resented that. I never found out which one of them turned Lev in. So, when your father came to me, I advised him to hide in the forests and try to stay hidden and away from the city. I hoped he would be able to survive that way. I never heard from him again."

"My mother? Have you heard from my mother, or have you heard anything about Gilde?"

"Nothing. Nothing about either one. As I said, I tried to write to Gilde, but there was no answer, and two of my letters were returned unopened."

"I tried, too. Mine were returned as well. You heard nothing of Mother?"

"That day she went to the police station to find your father was the last day any of us ever saw or heard from her."

"Oh, Lotti. You can't imagine how many times I've wished I could talk to her. I was so hard on her. If only I could tell her how much I love her. When I was young, I didn't understand everything she went through, and I was always ready to judge her for her mistakes. Now I've lived, and I know how things can happen to people, and circumstances can force you to do things you aren't proud of but had to do to survive. If only I'd told her I loved her before she left for the jail to find Papa. If only I'd said those words…"

"She knew you loved her," Lotti said, her voice kind and comforting as Alina remembered it as a child. Then Lotti tenderly patted Alina's hand. "Your mother always knew."

"Are you sure? Are you sure, Lotti?"

"Yes. I am positive. She and I talked about you. It was hard for you to understand everything that happened between her and your father. She understood that you were young. But, know this, she knew you loved her, and your mother loved you very much."

"Mama," Alina whispered under her breath, shaking her head. Alina was still on her knees on the floor. She put her head in Lotti's lap, and Lotti patted her hair. "I miss my family," Alina said.

"I know. I miss them, too. I miss everyone and everything about our lives before the Nazis. Hitler stole it all from us. He stole the joy from our little world. We did nothing to him. We did nothing to any of them."

"No, it was just hatred. The Nazis were consumed with it. Hatred needs no reason. And the Nazis had no reason."

Lotti nodded as she patted Alina's hair again. Alina felt warm and safe for a few minutes, like a child in Lotti's arms. Lotti was the only connection Alina had to the past. In Lotti's arms, Alina could feel a connection to her mother.

"I volunteer at a displaced persons camp. Every time I am working there, I see lost people in search of their loved ones. They are broken souls, emaciated, and alone. And as I look at them, I think to myself, 'So, this is the result, the end result of the powerful Third Reich that was supposed to save Germany.'"

"It destroyed Germany, but not only Germany. It destroyed so many other countries, too. And so now, those of us who are still alive must spend forever carrying the painful unanswered questions of what became of our friends and families. Also, we must live with the knowledge that so many innocent people died needlessly."

"Do you have any idea how I might go about looking for my parents?"

"No, Alina. I wish I did. There is nothing you can do. I've been looking for them. In fact, I've registered everywhere. No one can find any information," Lotti stated, shaking her head.

Alina nodded. "I am going to run ads in the London newspapers to see if I can find Gilde."

"That's a good idea. It would be so wonderful to find Gilde again," Lotti said. "Do you still remember when you and I worked at the orphanage together?"

"Yes, of course I do."

"I often think of those children. I wonder what happened to all of them. How many did we send on the Kindertransport?"

"I can't remember the exact number, but we sent all the children from the orphanage." Alina sighed. "It was so difficult for us to get them to take Gilde on the transport. For a while, I was afraid they wouldn't allow her to go. And then you, Lotti, you worked your magic. Everyone loved you. And even though Gilde wasn't technically one of the orphans, you somehow managed to get her in."

"Oh, you make me sound like I'm something special." Lotti laughed. "I wonder how many of those children survived." Lotti's face became somber. "With all of the bombing in London…"

Neither of them said what they were thinking, but both had grave looks on their faces when their eyes met, and both were silently asking. Is Gilde alive?

Alina got up from the floor. "I'll start the water for tea," she said, and once it was ready, she prepared a tray with the tea and cookies and carried it to the living room. After almost forty minutes, she remembered she had to introduce Lotti to Joey and Ugo.

They spent a few hours talking, reminiscing, and laughing. Lotti hugged Joey. She played with him and mentioned how much he looked like Johan. Her eyes glazed over with tears, but even so, while Lotti was playing with her nephew for a few minutes, Alina thought she could see a shadow of Lotti's younger self.

Alina and her family spent a week with Lotti. It was a glorious but, at the same time, sorrowful time for Alina. She and Lotti were close again, as close as they had been before the war. But it was hard to be in Berlin, in Lotti's apartment, and not think of her parents and sister. The reality of their absence was a constant reminder of all she'd lost.

And then it was time to go. Ugo had a business to run, and they had to return to America.

"Why don't you come to America with us? You can stay with us until you get on your feet. We'll apply for papers. You can start over, Lotti. In a new country."

"Yes, please come," Ugo echoed Alina. "I want you to know you are welcome in our home."

Lotti shook her head. "Thank you for the offer. But, no. I must stay here, right here, in this little apartment, and wait. Perhaps your parents or your sister will find their way back here. I wouldn't want them to come only to discover I had gone away. You see, leaving here would mean I've given up hope. And I will never give up hope."

"Yes, once the Nazis surrendered, I could finally see a glimmer of hope for my family," Alina said.

"I'm glad you came. Will you come back?" Lotti asked.

"I will. I will," Alina said. She took Lotti into a bear hug.

forty-five
Gilde

London
July 1946

VICKY'S INJURY took a toll on Gilde. The child was out of sorts, uncomfortable, and had limited mobility, so Gilde was forced to postpone her students' recital for a few months while Vicky was recovering. However, once Vicky recovered, Alden took a day off to care for her while Gilde's class had their long-awaited performance.

Because Vicky was young, her bones healed easily, but the incident made Gilde very protective of her daughter. She hovered over Vicky all the time as she blamed herself for her child's pain and suffering.

Being with Alden was like a dream. When they were apart, she believed she had lost him forever. And now that he was back, she cherished every precious day they shared.

When Alden proposed, Gilde was thrilled.

Gilde and Alden got married for a second time at a simple civil ceremony with Vicky at their side.

But because she was afraid to leave Vicky, Gilde wasn't keen to go on a honeymoon. Alden wanted to get away from the city so they could be alone together. Therefore, he convinced Gilde that he knew a nurse who would be happy to earn the extra money and could be trusted to watch Vicky closely. Finally, Gilde agreed.

The couple decided to go out to the beach in Brighton for a quiet, romantic weekend. They took the train out to Brighton and checked into a quaint hotel. For two days, they did very little. They just ate, walked the beach, and made love. Gilde was never so happy, and except for the phone calls to London to inquire about Vicky, they had no contact with the outside world. On the second morning of their vacation, Alden and Gilde woke up in each other's arms. The passion stirred, and they made love. After they had finished, they lay in bed watching the sun flicker through the window.

"Are you sure you don't miss the theater?" he asked gently, rubbing her shoulder.

"I'm sure."

"You know I am not going to tell you what to do about the school. You can keep the school open or not. It's your choice, but I earn enough money to take care of us," he said.

"I think I am ready to close it. I needed something to bridge the gap between leaving the theater and losing you in my life. Now, I would like to concentrate on being a wife and mother. That's where my heart is."

"Are you happy?"

"Very happy, Alden, are you?"

"You don't know how happy I really am."

"So, why don't you show me?" she said.

He took her into his arms, and they made love again. Afterward, they both fell asleep and didn't awaken until the afternoon.

forty-six
Gilde

WHEN THEY RETURNED from their honeymoon, Gilde and Alden walked into their flat to find the nurse sitting quietly in the living room, rocking Vicky, who slept peacefully in her arms. The house was clean and in perfect order. Gilde was relieved to see that Vicky was fine. Since the accident, she was always on guard.

As the days passed, Gilde finally felt at peace in her life. She'd always been searching for something. But now she had finally stopped seeking. She knew exactly what she wanted and where she wanted to be.

It was wonderful to see how much Alden had missed Gilde and Vicky. It was apparent in everything he did—small gestures like bringing home little treats for Vicky, candy or flowers for Gilde, to larger, more life-altering decisions like putting money away every pay period to buy a house for the family.

One day, as Alden was on the floor playing with Vicky, Gilde watched him from the kitchen. He had no idea that he was being observed. She saw him hold Vicky to his chest for several minutes. Then, lean his head on her tiny head. It was a tender moment that touched Gilde deeply. She put her hand to her lips as she continued to watch. But Vicky got bored and fidgeted, so Alden lifted her high in the air until she giggled.

His eyes were fixed on Vicky as he smiled up at her.

Gilde walked into the room. "I love the sound of her laughter."

"Yes, so do I. She's growing so fast, " Alden said.

"I know. I can't believe it. She is so active now."

"God, I am glad to be home." He sighed. "You know, Gilde, I am sorry for being so selfish. I was thinking about it the other night."

"About what?"

"Well, you know, I felt ignored and, well, like I wasn't important to you when you were in the theater. But the truth is that I have asked you to be understanding of my career. I work long hours, and I cannot always be at home. But I hope you never feel second best."

She shook her head. "I don't."

"I don't really know how to say this. But, if you want to return to the theater, I will stay with you, and we'll work it out. I don't want to live without you. But I don't want you to be unhappy either."

"I don't want to go back, Alden. This is what I want. You, Vicky, our home…"

"I really do love you," he added, "more than you'll ever know."

Gilde smiled at him. "Too bad we can't leave her for a few hours. I'd love to be in your arms."

Alden looked at her, and she could see the desire in his eyes. "You know, you have always had the power to do that to me. You could always make me forget all my responsibilities and want nothing more than to make love to you."

"But she is far too active to leave alone. After that accident…"

"No, you're right. Not now. Later tonight, she will be asleep when I get home from work. Then it will be our time."

He still worked long hours. But he never volunteered for extra shifts. In fact, he couldn't wait to get home.

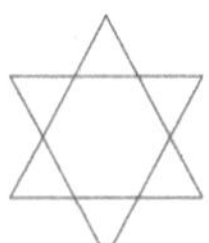

forty-seven

Gilde

"YOU BROUGHT HOME A CHRISTMAS TREE? Where did you get it?"

"I bought it from some fellow who cut down trees for firewood." He laughed.

"I'd like to light a menorah, too. I would like Vicky to grow up knowing that her parents are both Jewish and Christian."

"Well, then, let's do it. Alden smiled. "Do you have a menorah and the candles?"

"I have a menorah from when I was married to William. I'll have to buy candles," Gilde said.

Together, they tried to explain the holidays and what they meant to Vicky. She was too young to understand, but she was giddy with excitement because of the decorations on the tree and the sparkling wrapped gifts underneath.

Hannukah began on December 17, a cold and snowy night. Gilde and Alden would light the menorah for the next eight days, and then Christmas would fall on the eighth night of Hannukah. Each night, Alden and Gilde gave Vicky a small toy. She picked up on her parents' playful attitude and tried desperately to spin a dreidel on the kitchen floor. Then, on Christmas, Alden came home early from work with a bundle in his arms.

"What's this?" Gilde asked. She was standing at the stove preparing a special dinner. Vicky was napping.

"This, my love, is a new friend. Someone special for Vicky to grow up with. I should probably have asked you first. I hope it's all right. But every child should have a dog, don't you think?"

Gilde looked into his eyes. She was puzzled. She hadn't been expecting this. After wiping her hands on a kitchen towel, she pulled the blanket open, and inside, she found a small yellow puppy. Her tail was wagging, and if dogs could laugh, this one was laughing.

"Oh my gosh. Let me see this little fellow," Gilde said, taking the puppy from Alden's arms.

"You like her?"

"I love her. How could you not love her? She's adorable. What's her name?"

"Whatever you want it to be."

"Vicky will be so thrilled. But Vicky isn't the only one who will be happy. I like her too."

When Vicky woke up and saw the dog, she squealed with delight. The puppy instantly knew Vicky would be a great friend and began licking Vicky's face.

"How about Pal? I had a dog named Pal when I was young," Alden said.

"Pal. Yes, I think so. She certainly looks like she will be quite the pal for Vicky."

Then that night, when Vicky finally went to sleep with her arms around Pal, Alden and Gilde were alone.

"I'm glad you got her a dog. Got us a dog." Gilde said.

"I'm glad you're not angry. I can't really take credit for planning it. Some fellow came into the hospital carrying the puppy. He said he had to get rid of her. The staff didn't want any part of the situation. But when I saw that little ball of yellow fur, well, Pal melted my heart," Alden said.

"Of course, I'm not mad."

"Oh, I forgot something." He smiled at her and winked. "Just sit here a minute," Alden said. Then he went into his overcoat pocket and took out a small box. "This is for you, my love."

"For me, Alden?"

Gilde took the box and opened it. Inside was a gold ring inlaid with tiny diamonds. "Oh, Alden, it is beautiful. I wasn't expecting you to bring anything for me. I always thought holidays were for children."

"Holidays only give us extra reasons to celebrate our love. Not only our love for children but our love for each other," he said. Then he took the ring out of the box and put it on the fourth finger of her left hand. "It's a wedding ring, Gilde. I never gave you a wedding ring," he said.

She held the ring up to her heart and smiled through her tears.

"With this ring I thee wed…" Alden whispered.

forty-eight

Lotti

Berlin
December 1946

BY CHRISTMAS, Gabe had finished his tour of duty and returned home to America. He didn't ask Lotti to go with him. They had discussed it many times, and she had made it clear that she would never move away from the little apartment where she lived. And she'd also made sure that he knew that she would never regard their affair as anything but casual.

Gabe had explained that he wanted stability, a home, a wife, and a family. Lotti understood. But she told him that she could never be that for him. He came to see her the day before he shipped out for home. She held him in her arms and cried a little when they said goodbye.

Gabe looked into Lotti's eyes and felt his heart break. He would never forget this sweet German woman with a heart of gold. But his time in Germany was over, and he wanted to leave Berlin and go home. He missed his family and his friends, and damn if he didn't miss America.

Because Gabe's leaving had left such a void in her life, Lotti spent all her free time at the displaced persons' camp to fill the loneliness.

On the night of December 25, after a depressing Christmas Day alone in her apartment, Lotti attended a Hannukah service at the DP camp. It was a simple service where a rabbi who had survived Auschwitz conducted a candle lighting ceremony with a menorah that another one of the survivors had managed to hide and then recover after the war.

After the eight small candles were lit, everyone began to sing. It was amazing to Lotti to see a room full of people who had lost so much and suffered so greatly still able to express heartfelt joy for something as small as the flicker of candlelight on a menorah. These broken people who had lost everything were up clapping to the music. Those who were still able sang and danced. Children who had been near death in a camp, hiding, or hiding out in the forests only two years ago were now laughing as they spun homemade dreidels on the floor. The scene was so sad but hopeful that it brought tears to her eyes. She remembered a Hannukah she'd celebrated long ago with Lev. He'd always respected her religion, and she'd respected his.

In fact, because he knew it would make her happy, he'd bought a Christmas tree and went to church with her for Christmas. That same year, she'd gone to synagogue with him and the Margolis family for Hannukah. What a beautiful time it was then. But today was special too because on this Christmas, this very special day of hope, it was a small miracle the way that both holidays had fallen on the same day. The eighth day of Hannukah and Christmas Day. To Lotti, it felt like she and Lev were joining. She smiled at the thought and didn't realize that tears ran down her cheeks until an older man approached her and handed her his handkerchief.

"Here, you look like you might need this," he said.

He wasn't handsome. He was weathered, but he looked kind. His light brown hair was thinning. His skin was pockmarked. But his eyes were warm, and she saw a glow, a tiny flicker in them.

"My name is Myron," he said.

"I'm Lotti."

"You're not Jewish?" he said.

"How do you know?"

"I don't know, I am just asking," Myron said.

"No, I am not Jewish, but my husband was."

"He's gone?"

"Yes, he is gone. Murdered, like so many others."

"I'm sorry. My wife, too, she is gone."

"I'm sorry," Lotti said.

"Yes, we are all sorry. Maybe we will always be sorry. Or maybe the only thing we can do now is to start to live again. Who knows, right?"

She nodded.

"Even after all we have been through, there is still Hannukah. There are still candles and singing, right?"

Again, she nodded.

"Come sit with me; let's talk for a while."

Lotti sat at a table across from Myron, and they began to talk.

"I was a baker in Austria before the Anschluss. It was a beautiful country then, very beautiful, like a picture book. I had a nice business. I had a wife and a young son. Nu, so..." He threw his arms up.

"We weren't rich, but we were happy. Back then, we were worried about silly things, like who to invite for Passover dinner. You know. Then everything changed when we were deported to the Lodz ghetto. A terrible place, one dirty prison block, very dirty, no running water, no place for sewage. My family and I lived in one room with fourteen other people. The Nazis controlled all of the food, and there was hardly enough. We were starving. My Rosey was so skinny that I would feel a chill when I looked at her."

"Rosey was your wife?"

"Yes, that was my wife. God rest her soul. Rosey refused to eat most of the time. She gave her food to our son. She wanted to make sure our boy had plenty. I did that, too. In the winter, we were freezing, with no heat. Still, those years were better than what was to come. At least we were together. For four years, we lived in Lodz ghetto, and then my wife got very sick. I was so afraid. I didn't know how I would survive without her. I cried, and I bargained with God, I prayed constantly, and still, she died there, in my arms. I am pretty sure she had typhoid. Of course, she was never diagnosed by a doctor. She was just there with me one day, and the next, she was gone. I wanted to give up, but I couldn't because of our child. So, I tried to do what I could to save my son, but he was only eight years old. I heard people saying that they were liquidating the ghetto and sending us to a death camp. I believed it, and I still do. So, I took my son and traded all the valuables we had left with a man working on the black market. He helped us to escape. My son and I roamed Poland for six months, hiding like animals. Then, we were captured and sent to Auschwitz. When we arrived, my son and I were separated. I never saw him again."

There was a silence. "So now you know my story," he shrugged. "Tell me yours."

"My husband was a carpenter. He built furniture here in Germany. We also had a good life for many years before Hitler took over. He was Jewish; I wasn't. Our marriage was illegal, as you know. Anyway, he was arrested, and they murdered him."

Myron nodded. "Yes, the story is the same, with minor variations for many of us. My son, I can't find him. I think that's even worse. Because I don't know if he is alive or dead, and I cannot stop looking until I know for sure. I've traveled to every DP camp in Poland and Germany to find someone who might know something about what happened to him. I hoped maybe someone was in a camp with him, somewhere, but I have learned nothing, nothing at all. It's like he disappeared or never was at all."

"A lot of people are in that same position. I, too, am searching for my dear friends. But so far, without any luck."

"You know, Lotti, I am meeting you under a sort of false pretense."

"I'm not sure what you mean, Myron."

"It's just that I might not have told you the whole truth."

Lotti's back reared up, and she stared at him. Who was this man? She was suddenly afraid. "Are you a Nazi who is hiding? I know that they are here."

He belched out a loud belly laugh. "For God's sake, no. I am not a Nazi. I will explain. You know Mrs. Zitelbaum? So many people here in the camp are getting married. Starting families, embracing life, and starting over."

"Yes, I know that, but what is it you are keeping from me?"

"Well…" He hesitated. "Mrs. Zitelbaum spoke to me about you. She came to me and told me that you are a good, kind person. She suggested that maybe I should find a way to meet you. Perhaps she said you and I would be a good fit for each other. I feel so funny saying all of this. But you see, when I introduced myself, I was already watching you and looking for a way to talk to you. I should have told you the truth right away, but I was afraid you might feel funny knowing someone suggested that maybe we should get to know each other."

She smiled. "Oh, Mrs. Zitelbaum. You mean Sarah? I was here for her wedding when she married Abe last week," Lotti said.

"A wedding in a displaced persons camp. The orchestra played beautifully. It was very touching to see everyone embrace life. There was music, and there was love. Then Abe, the groom, turned to the crowd and took the wine glass the rabbi had given him. Before he smashed it, he made a toast. Did you hear him?"

"I did. It brought tears to my eyes," she said.

"I will never forget what he said. He looked out at all of us and smiled, then in a loud voice that sent chills up my spine, he said, 'To another breath, to another sunrise. To life.' Then, as is customary in a Jewish wedding, in case you don't know, he put the glass under his foot and stomped on it. It broke into a million pieces, representing the millions of years he and his wife will love each other. I have to tell you the truth. I don't know if this story about the breaking of the glass has a real religious meaning. But someone explained it to me like that when I was a young man, and I loved the idea of it. So, it is what I like to believe."

"I saw it. It was very touching. It made me believe that there is still hope."

"As long as we are alive, Lotti, there is hope." He patted her hand. "I have often wondered why I was spared when so many died. But I know that there must be a reason. God must have a special purpose for me."

"You are not bitter? You still believe there is a God?"

"I do. I saw his face many times," he said.

"Even in the camps?" she asked.

"Especially in the camps, Lotti."

"I've felt bitterness and raged at God plenty of times. But I still believe, too."

"So, Abe and Sarah Zitelbaum are friends of mine. Last week, I was talking to her, and she mentioned you. In fact, Sarah speaks so highly of you. She says you are good to her, and you have a big heart. In fact, she says she has never known you to be unkind to anyone. I am a good person, too, Lotti. I don't have much to offer you. Only my companionship and myself. But I would be a good husband. You would have a true friend in me."

"Is this a proposal of marriage?" Lotti looked at him.

He nodded. "Yes, a rather pathetic one, I am afraid. But I have plenty of time, and you don't have to say yes right away, but it's—maybe—better for both of us to try to start over together. It is no good being alone, Lotti. My bubbie used to say, 'No one should ever be alone. Only a stone should be alone.' Now, believe me, I know I will never take the place of your husband. But he would want you to have a friend in this world."

"That he would." She sighed. Lotti's heart ached for someone to share her life with, for a friend. Perhaps this was God's answer. "Yes," she said.

"Yes, you will marry me, or yes, you want more time?"

"Yes, I will marry you," she said.

He smiled. "Good. This will be good."

"Myron. Perhaps you should know. I can't have children."

"Me either. I was used by Dr. Mengele in an experiment that left me sterile. I was going to tell you about it..." He looked away from her, ashamed.

"No need to tell me if you don't want to, but I'll listen if you feel the need to talk about it."

"Maybe sometime. Not now. This is a happy time. We are going to get married, and then we'll get to know one another."

"It seems strange to do things this way, doesn't it?" Lotti asked him.

"Yes, it does. But these are strange times. Nothing is as it was before the Nazis and the war. So much loss, so much sadness. Nu? So what can you do? All you can do is look everywhere, even in the deepest, darkest corners, for just a little bit of happiness. And when you find a crumb, you grab onto it. Do you know what I mean?"

She nodded and swallowed hard.

forty-nine

Gilde

London
January 1947

"THIS PUPPY IS HARDER to paper train than I expected," Gilde said. "Did you get the newspapers on your way home from work, Alden?"

"Of course. They are in a pile on the dining room table," Alden said, taking her in his arms and kissing her.

"You're freezing. Sit down and have a cup of tea," Gilde said, walking into the kitchen to fill the kettle with water and begin heating it.

"Where is Vicky?"

"Napping with Pal right beside her. I get so infuriated with that dog, and then she does something cute, and I can't stay mad at her. Besides, Vicky just loves her."

"Yes, she does," Alden opened the newspapers to spread them out on the floor for the puppy to use to paper train. "Gilde?" He stopped and put the paper on the table. "Come here and look at this."

Gilde left the water on the stove. She walked over to Alden. "What?"

"This ad. I think this is your sister. Alina Margolis? That's your sister, isn't it?"

"Yes," Gilde said, grabbing the paper. "It says here that she is looking for me. Gilde Margolis. There is an address here in America where I can write to her. My sister is in America. Alina is alive!"

Alden reread it to be sure. "Yes, you are going to write to her?"

"Of course. I'll send her a letter with our telephone number," Glide said. "I'll do it right now. Oh God, Alden, you don't know how many times I tried to reach Alina or Lotti in Germany, but I haven't been able to get a letter through. I don't know what happened to Lotti and Lev or my parents. But Alina is in America!" Gilde's hand trembled as she held Alden's hand to her heart. Tears filled her eyes. "My sister is alive, Alden. Alina is alive."

fifty
The Gathering

New York
June 1947

IT WASN'T easy to convince Lotti and her new husband, Myron, to make the trip to America, but after much coaxing, Lotti agreed to accept money for passage from Alina.

Alina spoke to Gilde on the phone, and they cried, laughed, and cried some more. Then, they arranged for Gilde and Alden to bring Vicky to the United States for a visit.

For the first time since the war began, they would all be together again. Alina was excited and nervous. She and Ugo had sold Trevor's house and bought a home that was large enough for everyone to stay with them. She was nervous and eager to see her sister. The last time Alina had seen Gilde, Gilde was just a child.

The weather was beautiful. The rose garden Alina had planted along the fence was in bloom; the trees were overflowing with leaves, and the sun shone down as Ugo set up long tables in the backyard of their home. Alina had purchased all the food she could think of that Gilde and Lotti might enjoy.

Lotti arrived first, with Myron at her side. Alina embraced her old friend. She was glad that Lotti had finally agreed to come. Lotti didn't want to leave the old apartment because she still believed that Taavi and Michal would someday miraculously reappear. But at least Lotti had remarried, and she was no longer living a solitary life. Alina had strong doubts that her parents were still alive. But she would never tell that to Lotti. Instead, she embraced the sheer joy of being in her company.

Then Gilde, wearing a white dress with a print of red roses, her long golden hair caught up in a pearl comb, came walking through the door to Alina's house. She was holding Vicky in her arms. Alina looked at her sister and felt her knees tremble. She couldn't hold back the tears.

"My God, Gilde, the last time I saw you, you were so young. We were both shivering on the platform while waiting for the train. And here you are, all grown up and with a child of your own."

"I remember," Gilde said, tears running down her face.

Alina walked over to Gilde, and at first, the embrace was clumsy, but then they hugged tightly.

"I thought of you often," Gilde said.

"I thought of you too, Gilde, my little sister."

Then Lotti walked into the room, "Gilde! Oh, just look at you." Lotti hugged Gilde.

"This is Vicky, your niece." Alina touched Vicky's hair, but Vicky buried her head in her father's chest. "She's shy until she gets to know you," Gilde said.

"This is Joey, my son. Johan's son…."

"Joey…" Gilde said. At first, she couldn't hide the shock at Joey's broken body. Then Joey stumbled over to Gilde and hugged her.

"My mom told me all about you. She told me you were coming. I am so glad to meet you," Joey said, and Gilde's heart melted.

And so it was that these old friends who had suffered so much, who had starved and endured pain and suffering, finally ate their fill of good food.

They laughed and embraced and cried that summer day in America. They smiled at their memories of the good times before the war. They told funny, tender stories about Taavi, Lev, Johan, and Michal.

As they sat at that table bathed in sunshine, with the fragrance of roses wafting up from the garden, somewhere in another time, space reality, call it heaven, or whatever blessed place you like, Michal, Taavi, Johan, and Lev watched their loved ones, and they smiled.

The End

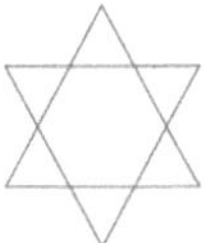

a note from the author

Dear All,

I always enjoy hearing from my readers, and your thoughts about my work are very important to me. If you enjoyed my novel, please consider telling your friends and posting a short review on Amazon. Word of mouth is an author's best friend.

Also, it would be my honor to have you join my mailing list. As my gift to you for joining, you will receive 3 **free** short stories and my USA Today award-winning novella! To sign up, just go to my website at... www.RobertaKagan.com

I send blessings to each and every one of you,
Roberta

Email: roberta@robertakagan.com

about the author

I wanted to take a moment to introduce myself. My name is Roberta, and I am an author of Historical Fiction, mainly based on World War 2 and the Holocaust. While I never discount the horrors of the Holocaust and the Nazis, my novels are constantly inspired by love, kindness, and the small special moments that make life worth living.

I always knew I wanted to reach people through art when I was younger. I just always thought I would be an actress. That dream died in my late 20's, after many attempts and failures. For the next several years, I tried so many different professions. I worked as a hairstylist and a wedding coordinator, amongst many other jobs. But I was never satisfied. Finally, in my 50's, I worked for a hospital on the PBX board. Every day I would drive to work, I would dread clocking in. I would count the hours until I clocked out. And, the next day, I would do it all over again. I couldn't see a way out, but I prayed, and I prayed, and then I prayed some more. Until one morning at 4 am, I woke up with a voice in my head, and you might know that voice as Detrick. He told me to write his story, and together we sat at the computer; we wrote the novel that is now known as All My Love, Detrick. I now have over 30 books published, and I have had the honor of being a USA Today Best-Selling Author. I have met such incredible people in this industry, and I am so blessed to be meeting you.

I tell this story a lot. And a lot of people think I am crazy, but it is true. I always found solace in books growing up but didn't start writing until I was in my late 50s. I try to tell this story to as many people as possible to inspire them. No matter where you are in your life, remember there is always a flicker of light no matter how dark it seems.

I send you many blessings, and I hope you enjoy my novels. They are all written with love.

Roberta

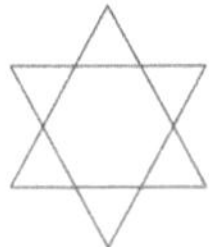# more books by roberta kagan

Available on Amazon

Margot's Secret Series

The Secret They Hid

An Innocent Child

Margot's Secret

The Lies We Told

The Blood Sisters Series

The Pact

My Sister's Betrayal

When Forever Ends

The Auschwitz Twins Series

The Children's Dream

Mengele's Apprentice

The Auschwitz Twins

Jews, The Third Reich, and a Web of Secrets

My Son's Secret

The Stolen Child

A Web of Secrets

A Jewish Family Saga

Not In America

They Never Saw It Coming

When The Dust Settled

The Syndrome That Saved Us

A Holocaust Story Series

The Smallest Crack

The Darkest Canyon

Millions Of Pebbles

Sarah and Solomon

All My Love, Detrick Series

All My Love, Detrick

You Are My Sunshine

The Promised Land

To Be An Israeli

Forever My Homeland

Michal's Destiny Series

Michal's Destiny

A Family Shattered

Watch Over My Child

Another Breath, Another Sunrise

Eidel's Story Series

And . . . Who Is The Real Mother?

Secrets Revealed

New Life, New Land

Another Generation

The Wrath of Eden Series

The Wrath Of Eden

The Angels Song

Stand Alone Novels

One Last Hope

A Flicker Of Light

The Heart Of A Gypsy